Long Road to the
CIRCUS

BETSY BIRD

Long Road to the CiRCUS

Illustrations by

DAVID SMALL

Alfred A. Knopf

New York

Text copyright © 2021 by Elizabeth Bird
Jacket art and interior illustrations copyright © 2021 by David Small

All rights reserved. Published in the United States by
Alfred A. Knopf, an imprint of Random House Children's Books,
a division of Penguin Random House LLC, New York.

Knopf, Borzoi Books, and the colophon are registered trademarks of
Penguin Random House LLC.

Photos of Madame Marantette courtesy of the Archives of St. Joseph County Historical
Society of Michigan.
Photo of Jimmy Winkfield © Kentucky Derby

Visit us on the Web! rhcbooks.com

Educators and librarians, for a variety of teaching tools,
visit us at RHTeachersLibrarians.com

Library of Congress Cataloging-in-Publication Data
Names: Bird, Betsy, author. | Small, David, illustrator.
Title: Long road to the circus / Betsy Bird; illustrated by David Small.
Description: First edition. | New York: Alfred A. Knopf, 2021. | Audience: Ages 10
& up. | Audience: Grades 4–6. | Summary: Twelve-year-old Suzy Bowles dreams
of life outside the small town of Burr Oak, Michigan, but when she stumbles on
the opportunity to learn ostrich-riding with the infamous Madame Marantette, her
obligations to her family on the farm threaten to derail her dreams of a bigger life.
Includes photographs and information on Madame Marantette.
Identifiers: LCCN 2020050918 (print) | LCCN 2020050919 (ebook) |
ISBN 978-0-593-30393-1 (hardcover) | ISBN 978-0-593-30398-6 (library binding) |
ISBN 978-0-593-30399-3 (ebook)
Subjects: CYAC: Ostriches—Fiction. | Circus performers—Fiction. |
Family life—Fiction.
Classification: LCC PZ7.B5118798 Lo 2021 (print) | LCC PZ7.B5118798 (ebook) |
DDC [Fic]—dc23

The text of this book is set in 10-point Melior LT Pro.
The illustrations were created using pen and ink.
Interior design by Martha Rago

Printed in the United States of America
October 2021
10 9 8 7 6 5 4 3 2 1
First Edition

For Mom and Aunt Judy:

"Our rags may flap us to death, but we will not starve."

Thank you for your stories.

—B.B.

To Sarah

—D.S.

Long Road to the
CiRCUS

One

"Strongest grip in a girl I've ever saw," Daddy said, not without some pride.

I looked down at my palms, rubbed raw where earlier I'd clung to the elm tree in our front yard with my no-good, stinking brother Bill pulling on my leg to get me down. He'd called me in for mealtime and I didn't want to jump to obey his word, so there'd been a good five minutes of yanking and gripping before Daddy put a stop to it. I still wasn't feeling anything in four of my fingers, but his praise was a cool, clear salve to those burning digits. A salve, that is, until Mama chimed in with "Just like the day she was born."

Once she said that, no amount of moaning on my part

could derail her from telling "The Legend of Baby Suzy," and believe me, I'd tried. Changing the subject didn't amount to anything. Lying about our cow going into labor didn't do any good (possibly because she wasn't pregnant at the time). Ignoring my petulance, Mama launched right in.

"The day you were born, lamb pie, you gave me more trouble than I'd ever had with your sister and brothers." This was no small thing. Mama had three kids before me, and according to her, each one had been a trial. "I thought I knew all the ins and outs of birthing, but you gave me a real ride. You just didn't want to leave! You were holding on for dear life to keep from meeting the world." Then she began to laugh.

My mama cannot talk about the day I was born without bursting into giggles. Granny says it's unseemly. That means whenever she gets to the hilarious part, Granny will totter over and start poking her with her cane, which only sets my mama off further.

"Get ahold of yourself, woman!" Granny says. "Birthing babies is our war! And telling the stories of it means telling about all the bloodshed and battles we overcame. Ain't no time for tittering like a schoolchild." Then she'll poke me once with the cane and say, "You don't see this one acting the fool when you tell that tale."

I don't think it much fair to get rammed in the head

when I am doing something she likes, but that's the way with Granny. Doing something right gets you one poke. Doing something wrong gets you a lot worse.

Anyway, the reason I wasn't guffawing along with the rest of the family is because I've never found the story all that funny. And that's on account of how Mama ends the story.

"Finally we get you out and there you are, smaller than a coop's egg. This tiny little baby, all flailing limbs and wailing cry, looking half-starved, which is not the way a baby should be. But quick as lightning you latched on and started drinking on me, from the get-go. That's when we knew you would do just fine."

A pause.

"Except—"

"Except nothing," I interrupted, not eager to hear any more. "And I ate everything you ever put in front of me and stayed small and that's okay, the end."

"Except," she continued, like she hadn't heard me, "when your granny came in to take you so I could rest—and truth be told, I was pretty tired as well—we tried to dislodge your tiny baby hands from my hair and clothes, and discovered a grip we'd never encountered before. Strongest thing I've ever felt from something that small."

"Could be you just didn't try hard enough," Granny muttered to herself.

Mama shrugged at that. "I was plumb exhausted, I admit," she said. "But the harder I tried, the harder you'd grip."

Every single time, without fail, she'd start to laugh again. Laughing at the remembrance of laughing.

"There's Granny looming over me, trying to take the baby Suzy away, and I just couldn't get you loose. And then suddenly"—she snorted, which isn't ladylike, but at this point she didn't care—"I'm laughing too hard to dislodge you."

"And then Granny gives it a try," Daddy continued, because by this time Mama was having a high old gigglefest and wasn't fit to talk, "and she can't get you to let go either."

"I tried," Granny snapped. "But as soon as you got one hand undone, the other one would snake up and grab whatever was in reach." She glared long and hard at me. "Like she was doing it on purpose."

Not having anything to say to that, I said nothing.

Now Daddy was laughing too, along with my siblings. Even Bill was laughing, but that's because he's a nasty toad of a brother, and that look on his face wasn't because he found the story funny but because he found my finding the story not funny, funny. Make sense?

"And then I tried to pull," Daddy said, "and you just gripped your mama harder. I thought we'd have to take scissors to the dress just to cut you off."

"And my hair!" Mama cackled.

Oh, they're a regular funny troop, my family. I stood to leave, but Mama's hand shot out and grabbed me. And if there's any question of who I get my grip from in this family, they just need to feel that vise. You go nowhere.

"The thing is," she said, calming down slowly and looking at me with real love, "I knew then that you were going to be one of my best and biggest problems, right from the start. Knew it like I knew your pretty face. 'Cause my girl's the kind who never lets go of something when she wants it. Never."

"Any fool can grip," Granny spat. "It's the smart ones that know when to let go."

Well, there you have it. My name is Suzy Bowles and I've never known when to let go a day of my life.

Two

Let me tell you something about the summer of 1920 in Burr Oak, Michigan. So far it had been a nice round year with not a lot happening. In fact, I had good reason to suspect that as summers went, this one was shaping up to be among the dullest. President Woodrow Wilson was in office, but according to Mama and Daddy, he wasn't doing a whole lot of stuff, and that's just the way they liked it. Unfortunately, the very stuff he wasn't doing was causing some problems for our farm. Seemed like a lot of folks in town were out of work, which was just weird to me, seeing as in farm country, land's all around. Someone has to till it. What was stopping them?

Case in point, Uncle Fred. Wait. Stop. I got that all wrong.

According to our neighbors and friends and pretty much any lady I've ever passed on the street for the better part of my short life, his name is actually Lazy Old Fred or Good Ole No-Good Fred or even Deadbeat Fred, which has a nice ring to it alongside its not-too-nice meaning. Uncle Fred was one of those folks out of work. That wouldn't have been much of anything except, somehow, he was married now with a kid, and if he didn't work and his wife didn't work and the baby didn't work (naturally), then nobody was working and everyone was starving. Plus, he was Daddy's brother and all, so the solution seemed simple. Uncle Fred was gonna come to our farm to be a farmhand. Not much in the way of pay, but free food and a place to sleep. Not too shabby.

Our farm's pretty good as they go. It's not all that big. We've only got a few cows and chickens and horses and sometimes a goat or a pig or a sheep or two, but the crops are decent and that's where Daddy and his hired crew spend most of their time. That's where Uncle Fred was going to spend his time too, when he came. Which he did in just the strangest way.

I wasn't paying all that much attention when Uncle Fred, Aunt Juliet (that's his wife), and little Catalonia stumbled onto our property. Someone had mentioned they were coming, but I don't think I heard it at the time on account of the fact that my brother Bill kept whispering to me all breakfast that there was no way I was gonna be able to keep that toad I'd caught the day before. Bill's two years older than me, and he's the closest to my age on the farm. The rest of my siblings are all okay. I keep out of their way and they keep out of mine. Except Bill. I know we're supposed to love our brothers like ourselves (which they say in church ALL the time), but there ain't no way to love Bill. He is unlovable. Something's not right with him. Mama loves him, but I think she's the only one who does. Daddy pays so much more attention to Ernest, who's big and strong and does what he's told, that he ignores Bill half the time, and for the other half he's yelling at him for some prank he pulled or job he didn't do. It's what makes the boy such a mean son of a gun. Or why he's the worst to me. Particularly when it comes to pranks involving food and slimy worms.

Now, if it happened to anyone else, I might almost admire Bill for managing to get five of those crawlers onto a single breakfast plate without anyone seeing. The problem was, it was *my* plate, and under usual circumstances I really, really like Mama's scrambled eggs. Then there's the fact that I came dangerously close to shoveling one of those thick, bluish worms right down my gullet, and it's a miracle I saw the telltale wiggle in time.

I've found that when it comes to handling Bill, actions speak louder than words. That's why I perched myself on the porch roof when he wasn't looking and then balanced one hand down on the trellis. With my feet hooked on a strong-but-loose roof tile, I was in the perfect striking position. My mission was one of revenge.

I imagine the scene that met my uncle, aunt, and tiny cousin as they came up the drive that day was probably as close to a full-blown family carnival as they had ever hoped to see. There I was, the lower half of me on the porch roof and the upper half gripping the trellis with one hand and Bill's ear with the other. It's a pity they hadn't seen my lunge. I'd whipped out fast, like a water moccasin nabbing a frog, and Bill was howling practically before I started digging my fingernails into him.

"NEVER PUT STUFF IN MY FOOD AGAIN!" I screamed at him. He was doing his own fairly good worm imitation, writhing and wiggling under me, but I'd wedged my feet so well into the roof that I wasn't budging for anything. Besides, he knew my hands don't let go until I tell 'em so. Each one of my joints has a little lock in it, and only I know the combination.

"I won't do it again, I promise!" he howled, but we both knew he was lying.

"Actually promise!" I howled right back, but by now he'd seen our relatives standing, shocked, at the bottom of the stairs. He stopped caterwauling all of a sudden, and, confused, I strained my neck to see what the heck had distracted him from my vengeance.

"Ah, hello," said the man. He was a raw-boned, unhappy-looking fellow. All hunched up at the top and floppety down below. His wife was pretty but looked like she was just half a second from getting old too soon. And the baby? They pretty much all look the same to me until they're able to string four words together.

Bill took advantage of my surprise and managed to pry my thumb and forefinger apart for half a second before I felt what he was doing and double-quick grabbed him again. He screamed bloody murder, and then the rat appealed to the man standing before us.

"Please, Uncle Fred, save me!" he said.

Uncle Fred? I'd heard Daddy talk about him for years but had never seen him in the flesh before now. He was what they call the outcast in the family or something. One of those fellows born here in Burr Oak who took off for parts unknown all around the country. To hear Daddy and Granny tell it, he was never satisfied in one place. Just kept bouncing and bouncing all over until, with all that bouncing, he somehow found himself a wife and child. Looked like he was finally bouncing back here again.

I vowed at that moment to find out more about the man. I had a boring summer before me. Might as well solve a tiny mystery or two.

Bill continued to whine. "Tell her to let go."

Uncle Fred looked me dead smack in the eyes and said, "Suzy. Let go of your brother now." I looked back, feeling defiant, but he hadn't said it in a mean or superior way. Just a conversational manner that made you think twice about being a hooligan in his presence. I dropped the ear, Bill went like lightning into the house, and Aunt Juliet looked plumb frightened by the whole ordeal.

"Juliet, why don't you take Catalonia into the house to meet my ma?" Uncle Fred said. "She'll be happy to welcome you when you do."

Aunt Juliet gave just the barest of nods, then ducked her head and scurried into the house. I wondered if she spoke at all or if she was more of the nodding and scurrying type. Takes all kinds.

Uncle Fred, for his part, just looked up at me, dropped his head, then settled down onto the top step of the porch.

"Need your help, girl, if you're able." No more words after that. Curious, I scrambled down the trellis and stood before him. When

he saw me, it was like he knew I'd come no matter what. Then he pointed to the top of his back on his right side.

"Saw you have strong hands. I've got a knot so big I can hardly lift my arm right now. Need you to pound it away with whatever strength you have." He paused. "Give you a nickel if you do."

My eyes brightened. A nickel! For doing to Uncle Fred's back what I'd done to my brother's ear for free? Without a word, I bounded up the porch steps and looked where he'd been pointing. As I did, I thought back to some of the off-handed comments I'd heard my daddy make about his brother over the years. "Can't hold on to his money for two minutes without it burning him," he'd say. "It's like his skin boils on contact with good honest cash. The minute he has it, he just has to get rid of it." Then he'd shake his head and give this little laugh like it was kind of cute, even if it drove him wild. "That man's never happier than when he's broke."

"Right there," Uncle Fred said, taking me out of my reverie. He was wearing just a thin blue shirt under his overalls, and I could see the lump. When I touched it, it felt like pure steel embedded under the skin.

"What do I do again?" I asked him.

He shrugged, as much as he was able. "Pound it. Move it. Break it up in some way. I don't care how you do it, but make it less than it is."

I didn't start at first. Just eyed the muscle, its contours and edges. Then, without warning, I plunged both hands in. Daddy says I get my finger strength not from any secret muscles or anything but from how bad I want whatever it is I'm holding on to. He says anyone can hold on to something, but few folks care like me. In Uncle Fred's case, I was more interested in the challenge of it. I always helped Mama knead the dough when it was a bread day. Uncle Fred's back was like that, only made of rock, not yeast and flour.

When Granny came out a few minutes later with little Catalonia in her arms (she'd probably eaten Aunt Juliet for breakfast and was taking a break before dining on the babe for dessert), I heard Granny inhale sharply. There sat Uncle Fred, gripping his knees, teeth clenched, trying not to cry while my fingers dove deep into the very heart of that foul muscle, shaping it into an all-new form. I could tell it hurt him from the amount of sweat that was popping out all over his neck. With every push and pull to his skin, I made the knot just a tiny bit smaller. Enough so that when Granny shrieked "Child, what are you doing to your poor uncle?" I felt my work was already done.

"She's making it so's I can work another day, Mama," Uncle Fred gasped when he was able. From his pocket, he took out a dirty nickel, the most beautiful thing I'd encountered in a long while.

I turned to go inside, when Granny's right claw of a hand shot out, nabbed my prize, and pocketed it in her bosom before I could say so much as a boo.

"Hey!" I said, already having lost all hope. "That's mine!"

Granny gave me a long, calculated glare over her tiny little glasses. "Better had you thought of that before you attempted to remove your brother's ear."

I glared back but dropped my gaze almost immediately. You can't maintain eye contact with Granny too long or the blood in your veins'll start to run backwards. That's what my sister Mary says anyway, and Mary's not one to lie or exaggerate.

Last I saw of my uncle that day, he was taking his time to stand up to say hello to his mother. The bags under his eyes were purple feed bags of misery. Little wonder that he was known as Lazy Old Fred to everyone here in Burr Oak, Michigan.

Everyone, it would seem, but Madame Marantette, the local circus queen.

Three

It takes true skill to delay doing your chores. And my impatient brother Bill simply had no idea how to do it right. He usually tried to skip out after breakfast to run and play with the baby lambs or the goats or whatever it was he wasn't supposed to be doing. But if Bill had taken pointers from Uncle Fred, like I did, he would have realized that the first rule of chore skipping is to skip breakfast too. 'Cause once they've seen your face and weighed you down with food, you're less fleet of foot. They'll catch you before you can take two steps outdoors.

The second rule is to offer complete and utter bafflement when confronted. When Bill got collared in an attempted escape, he always just lied outright. I'd shake my head in wonder as he constructed some fabulous falsehood to cover up his crime, making it far worse for himself the further in he went. Uncle Fred took a much smarter tack. Whenever he'd return from wherever it was he'd been and my daddy started asking where he'd gone, Uncle Fred would have this look of complete bafflement on his face. Like he'd never even grown up on a farm or known how it worked. He'd offer some bland apologies to Daddy for inconveniencing him, then join everyone for lunch. Usually after that he'd go to work with the rest of the crew, working longer than the rest of them to make up his lost time, but next morning it would start all over again. He'd be gone before breakfast, Daddy swearing under his breath, the rest of us pretending not to notice, most of all Uncle Fred's wife and baby. Aunt Juliet hadn't said much at all since she'd arrived, and she never talked about anything regarding her husband. I often saw her drifting around the house doing various chores, lost in dream worlds of her own. I sometimes wondered what those worlds looked like. I hoped they were nice.

Thing was, I'd taken a kind of shine to my lag-about uncle. When you're second youngest to the end of your siblings, you sort of blend into the woodwork more than you'd like. Ernest, as the eldest child at seventeen, was helping Daddy and a crew of two other men who came on for the early-summer season. Mary, at sixteen, had more boys than she knew what to do with and seemed to delight in frightening Daddy with the sheer number of them pounding on our front door, asking to "pay a call" on his daughter. Fourteen-year-old Bill, of course, was enough trouble in his own right. He would often beg not to come along with Ernest and Daddy at their work in the fields, far preferring to stay close to home and tend to the animals all day. This ploy never worked, as Daddy would trot out some point about him failing to be enough of a man with his behavior in recent weeks. Of course, every time he was told this, he'd set a course for revenge, with me as his nearest victim. Bill never seemed to put together that the more bad behavior he displayed, the more he proved Daddy's point. As for Dotty, just five years of age, she was the baby of the family. That is, until little cousin Catalonia came along. Bereft of the full extent of Mama's attention, Dotty considered any number of attention-seeking behaviors. These ranged from constantly claiming there were ghosts in the privy (the price of Bill's love of telling her scary stories), to turning the clean sheets on the laundry line into tents, to periodically abducting the chickens for the world's least-refined tea parties. Many was the time I'd come out to bring her in for bedtime, only to find her stuffing some poor fowl into doll clothes never meant for wings.

In the midst of all of this, nobody was much thinking about twelve-year-old Suzy. Me. I told all of this to my best friend, Mimi Aynuk, after church that very week.

"Let me sort this out," Mimi said. She was a farm girl like me, though more enamored of dresses and frills than I had ever been. If I had my way, I'd be wearing overalls to church. My attempts had resulted in one of the few times when both Mama and Granny were united in their opposition. Sitting next to Mimi on the bench outside the church while our parents gabbed, I picked sullenly at the calico fabric poking up at my knee. Mimi cheerfully swatted my hand away as I identified a loose string, correctly deducing that I was mere seconds away from pulling it and freeing the lower half of my dress in the process.

"Your uncle," she continued, "who is not here at church, I might add . . ."

I looked about, which was sort of silly because I knew perfectly well that neither he nor any of his family had joined us in the wagon to church that day.

". . . is up to something."

I looked Mimi over real close. She was bigger than me (which isn't saying much because newborn baby colts are practically bigger than me), with wide, knowing eyes and a way of making her face look like she was revealing unto you the secrets of the universe. And half the time she was.

"What do you mean 'up to something'?" I pressed.

She ticked off the facts on her fingers. "Stands to reason. He's up before anyone else at daybreak." This was true. You had to get up pretty early in the morning to beat my mama starting her morning cooking. "He never says where he goes. And he goes every day. Up. To. Something."

I scratched my left ear and gave it some thought. "But where's he go?"

She shrugged. "Maybe he's got another lady?"

I cut her a glance. "Who visits a lady friend in the early morning?"

"Well, does he like to gamble or anything?"

I shook my head. "Need money to gamble. Uncle Fred never has two nickels to rub together." I thought nostalgically for a moment of my own nickel, lost forever in the depths of Granny's bosom. "Besides, again, who gambles in the morning?"

Mimi considered this and nodded. "Well then, maybe he's just lazy and likes to watch the deer feeding in the meadows. I don't know!" Then a sly, sneaky grin snaked across her face. "But I know someone who can find out."

I wasn't touching this one with a ten-foot pole. "You got some secret spy out there who can find all this out?"

"I got something better. I got you."

"I'm sorry. Piece of wool must've gotten stuck in my ear. Sounded like you just called me a spy."

"*You* called you a spy," she pointed out. "I would say you were doing a service to your daddy and family."

I looked over to where Daddy was chatting with the other men, in his Sunday best. Uncle Fred looked tired all the time, but so did Daddy in his own way. It wasn't the kind of thing you normally noticed. He was strong and lively, laughing with his friends in a manner that definitely implied he was discussing his no-good little brother with them. But I'd seen a photograph of my daddy when he was a young man with big dreams. He wasn't that old, but farming has a way of carving out a space in your soul to let in the age.

I took time to consider Mimi's plan. I'll say this much: even if I was caught tailing Uncle Fred, it wasn't like the crime could compare to 1. what Dotty did this morning to the hanging laundry, 2. what Bill didn't do when he was asked to chop some wood, or 3. the intentions of that boy Mary'd had over the other night (skinnier than a string bean, with eyes that were almost all leer).

I looked at Mimi dead on. "I'm in," I said. She almost squealed in delight. "But"—I held out a finger—"I warn you. It's not gonna be interesting. Nothing in this town is interesting."

I was right about the second part. Burr Oak's about as dull as dishwater in a plain tin pan. But Uncle Fred wasn't staying in Burr Oak after he left the house. So I couldn't have been more wrong about the first.

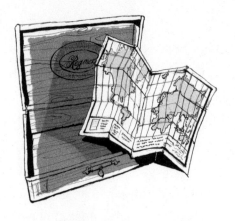

FOUR

I could see how some folks might have confused me with some kind of Goody Two-shoes, since the grown-ups yelled at me so rarely that when they *did* have to call my name, they usually had to say all my other siblings' names first in order to remember mine. "ErnestMaryBillDottySUZY! Come right over here!" Still, the fact of the matter is that I considered myself a much bigger problem than any of the other kids in the family. Not because I caused consternation with my every breath, but because of the consternation I was fixing to some-day bestow. My biggest secret, and the one I never told a soul, not even Mimi, was this: I had no intention of staying in this one-horse town.

And this dream was a really big deal. Granny was born in Burr Oak. When she was three, she sat on her daddy's shoulders and shook the hand of Abraham Lincoln himself as he passed through on the train line, campaigning for president. Something about that moment cemented in her mind the fact that Burr Oak was her past, her present, and her future. That'd be fine and all, but she made it clear that it was all *our* past, present, and futures too. Daddy had tried to get away. When he was a young man, he and his best friend went on a wild tour of the country, ending up in Oklahoma, where he'd found just the prettiest photographer's assistant he'd ever laid eyes on. Mama was cute and smart as a whip. He'd come into that photography studio hoping to get a picture taken to commemorate his trip, but when he left that town it wasn't just with a photograph but with a bride to match. Still, it was right straight back to Burr Oak they headed to raise a family and stay for all time. Heck, my eldest brother, Ernest, already had his eye on a girl in town he was sweet on.

After church that day, as I sat in Mary's room, hiding out from Bill and whatever mischief he hoped to make, she was gaga-ing and goo-goo-ing about the beanpole from the night before.

"Tell me you didn't think he was pretty cute, though," said Mary. Mary didn't have a lot of friends her age (which probably accounted for the proliferation of smitten menfolk), so more often than not she'd try to turn me into the friends she didn't have. This was one of those times, and it made me wish I could care two bits about boys.

"Mary," I said, moving the topic just an inch to the left, "can I ask you something about when you get married?"

"Of course!" She brightened. You can always ask Mary anything you like about lovey stuff.

I fidgeted with the buttons on my overalls. "Are you gonna stay in town when you get married or are you gonna go live somewhere else?"

She paused at her dressing table for a second, then picked up a brush and began brushing her hair. "Stay here, of course. Silly. Where else is there to be?"

"You never want to see anywhere else, then?" I looked out the window a little.

"Sure, I guess," she said. "Maybe honeymoon somewhere on Lake Michigan or something, but, honey, our whole family's here."

"Not Mama's family," I pointed out.

She laughed deep in her throat. "Oklahoma might be the moon for all we're ever seeing them. No, no. Your home is where your family is. What would happen if I was going to have a baby and I didn't have Mama and Granny to help me out? You gotta think practically when planning your future. Burr Oak has everything you need in it."

"I guess," I said. So I didn't tell her. Just excused myself and went to my room to think.

There was an old weak board under my bed, which I'd discovered one day when I was playing hide-and-seek. With a little pulling and prodding, I revealed a small space, just the perfect size for a cigar box. And so, when no one was looking for me, I'd slip under the bed, raise the board, and take out the box.

Now, Daddy gets his hands on a newspaper once a month or so, and then it pretty much gets used in the outhouse

after that. No one notices if a page or two goes missing. No one cares if the second-youngest daughter in the house sees something on those pages she wants to keep and look at. As I spread my clippings out before me, there didn't appear to be much rhyme or reason to the array. An article on the king of Spain's trip to American shores. Trade in China. Restaurants in San Francisco. A piece on the castles of France and how they fare today. And at the bottom of the cigar box, a yellowed, dusty map of the world, so small the countries on it were almost too tiny to make out. With it in hand, I lay under my bed, touched my fingers to it, and looked at that world.

I was no idiot. I knew the world was gigantic. But on that pressed pulp, it felt maybe like something I could handle. Sometimes I'd even take my palm and cover it all up. Whoop! There goes the world! The way I see it, if you can fit billions of people in your hand, then surely you can meet them someday. Living in a town not much bigger than this slip of paper, I knew everyone I saw. So I'd stare at those clippings and stare at the map and think of all the people there that I *didn't* know. I liked the feeling of my mind stretching to understand something that big. If I lived to be a thousand, how many of them could I meet? What could they teach me? If you keep meeting people, over and over, does it change your brain so that you're not you anymore? Does meeting more and more people make you a different kind of person? Someone who has something to look forward to beyond farming and babies and cleaning and cooking and chores?

If I meet lots of people, can I make myself one of them forever, instead of a me I already know?

In my family, you stay with family. But Mama left her family to try her hand in a new place. And then there was Uncle Fred. He left and came back again. Was it just to work for my daddy, or was there a different reason? Me, I wasn't just going to get out of town. I was going to get out of the country and see the world.

I just had to figure out how I was going to manage it first.

Five

There were lots of different methods for guaranteeing you'd get up before dawn's light, but none of them were surefire. Mimi and I had discussed a variety of options, but each one had a drawback. I could drink a gallon's worth of water the night before and count on my bladder to do the alarm clock business, but that was a sketchy matter at best. (Besides, I don't mind the outdoor privy during the day, but in the dark you can't make out the bitey spiders quite as well.) I could stay up all night, but that would make me too logy to do a proper following in the morning. I even thought about sneaking our rooster, Samuel, into my bedroom with me, but if he got me up, he'd get everyone else in the house up as well, with the possible exception of my little sister, Dotty. We shared a bed, but fortunately she's the kind of kid who sleeps like a small, loud log from sundown to sunrise. You could put thirty Samuels in bed with her, and for all their crowing she wouldn't even stir unless they bit her nose or something. It was one of the things I liked best about her, honestly.

In the end, I decided to half sleep it. Half sleeping is when you sleep, but in fits and starts. You just wake yourself up again and again and again all night. I was in luck that it was a moonlit night, so right after dinner I sneaked my father's pocket watch off the table where it was sitting. Then, after I went to bed, I made myself periodically check the watch all night. It wasn't a science, but I got pretty good at getting myself up at regular intervals. 8:10. 10:05. 11:48. 1:07. 2:45. 3:11.

4:25. I slipped out of bed and changed as silently as I could into my overalls. June air at night isn't freezing, but if you haven't slept proper, then there's this body chill you carry with you into the predawn air. I nabbed a sweater on my way out the door.

I had figured on crouching on the side of the porch to wait for Uncle Fred's departure, but when I exited the house, I had just enough time to see a man's loping form disappearing down the road off to the right. Dang it! The one time I was counting on my lazy uncle to live up to his reputation, and here he was acting like he had places to go and people to see.

With no time left to lose, I beat it lickety-split down the lane. My steps made a distinct pounding noise, so I ditched the road and leapt onto the grass on the side. The dew soaked my feet, and we were a long ways from sunny dawn. It was going to be a rough journey.

Uncle Fred was headed north or northwest by the looks of it. I kept to the ditches, but he was walking at a fair clip, and I knew I wouldn't be able to make up the lost time if I had to spend it fighting with the tall grass, chicory, and Queen Anne's lace every step of the way. I decided to take a risk and move back to the road instead. Uncle Fred never looked behind him, and the moonlight kept him lit enough that I didn't have any more trouble following.

We walked for a good hour and a half this way. Him never slowing. Me wondering where the heck we were and if we were going to be able to get back. I tried to make a mental map that could explain where we were going. It kinda reminded me of the route we'd take each year to the St. Joseph County Grange Fair. That was always my favorite time of year, with livestock shows and sweets and my favorite part of all, the parade. My heart quickened at the thought of the fair. Just two months until the next one. I could hardly wait.

Uncle Fred's route took us past countless farms and farmland. Great rolling fields, sometimes, and unkempt grassland alongside. It's pretty in its way. Some might call it beautiful. And some, like me, look at it and see the same people doing the same thing on the same strip of land year after year after year after year. Mama once said that when a person has been through something awful, they cling to things that don't change, like a drowning man clings to a rock jutting out of the sea. If everything stays the same, then they'll never feel unsafe again. I get that, I guess, but how to account for the people like me who wouldn't mind a little lick of danger once in a while? 'Cause I see that too. I see those kids, done with their farm chores, hanging around the town with nothing to cut the boredom out of their lives, getting into all kinds of mischief just because something in them is so desperate to see something different besides rolling hills and farms and more hills and more farms.

Not me, though. Following Uncle Fred was probably the most exciting thing I'd done in my whole life, and I was only doing it because I could already see what a dang-blasted boring summer I was doomed to have.

Finally Uncle Fred veered off the road, and in the

early-morning light I could just make out a large house in a field up ahead. A pasture and paddock ran alongside the road, but there were no trees in sight. I treaded as softly as I might so that he wouldn't see me. Of course, that was before I glanced to the side and saw something that almost made me yelp.

I'd pretty much lived by fields my whole life and knew what to expect of them. Cows, horses, sheep. The regulars. But what I was seeing here wasn't like anything I'd ever seen before. There, grazing as if it was the most normal thing in the world, was a herd of ostriches.

I counted. Twelve. Twelve full-grown ostriches, walking about. I'd always lived with chickens. Chickens get ruffled at you sometimes, and you can't really blame them for it (their own dang fault for being so tasty, really), but you don't *worry* about them. You don't stay awake at nights pondering whether they're going to gang up on you or anything. But staring now at these monsters, it was like I was seeing nature's revenge on behalf of poultry. They were huge.

But that's not what I found so strange, seeing them so close up. Not nearly. It was their necks. Like some fool took a snake or an elephant's trunk and, as a prank, stuck it between the body and the head of this poor creature. I could deal with the size. I could deal with the gait and their big blank eyes. But the way that neck moved just played kitty claws down my spine. Name me one thing in this good, great world important enough to justify a neck like that. One thing. Can't be done.

A sign hung on the wire fence around the birds, warning,

"NOTICE! Visitors Are Positively Forbidden to Feed the Ostriches!" A more unnecessary warning I have yet, in this life, to see.

Just like that, I knew where my uncle had been heading every day.

"If you're coming, you might as well see," Uncle Fred said. Not too loudly, but loud enough to be heard over the early-morning birdcalls.

I stopped in the road, cold. Then figured it made more sense to own up to the situation than let it continue. He waited, still not turning his head, as I approached. When I was up alongside him, I asked, "How long did you know I was there?"

He smiled then, and later I would recall that it was the first time I'd ever seen him do so. Still, his sad eyes didn't meet my own. "You're about as quiet as a jackdaw," was all he said.

We walked along the ostrich pasture, silent for a bit. I was having a hard time tearing my eyeballs away from the big birds. Unnervingly, a couple were walking alongside us, kind of like you do when you don't quite trust a person.

"Did you know that they're the largest birds that walk on land?" Uncle Fred said.

"Really?" I said. "And what's the largest bird that walks on the bottom of the sea?"

He made a sound that I took to be some kind of a laugh, with a snort at the end. I smiled all secret to myself.

The grand white house presented itself with a large open yard, and there, standing on the porch, was Madame Marantette herself.

You can't live in St. Joseph County and not have heard the rumors about the Madame. After all, not everyone has their own world-famous celebrity within riding distance. Every year, people would come from miles around to the St. Joseph County Fair parade to see just one thing. They'd stand alongside the parade route, anticipating the moment when they'd catch a glimpse of an unmistakable sight. With Madame Marantette, you'd always see the ostrich first, and then, tall as a tree, sharp as a sapling, there she'd be, pulled in her surrey. She'd sit there, like a queen in her carriage, and what could have been funny or even ridiculous instead had the trappings of royalty and nobility about it. I had always kind of wondered about her. Funny thing was, I didn't know if what I'd picked up about her over the years was true or not. Former circus queens make for some pretty wild tales. The one thing that seemed certain was that she'd traveled the world once. What I couldn't figure was why she ever moved here. If you're gonna conquer the world, what's it all for if you just wind up in the middle of nowhere?

Sometimes, when you get to meet someone larger than

life, the experience can be a bit of a disappointment. You approach your heroes only to find them picking their nose on the sly. But as I came up that drive alongside Uncle Fred, the Madame loomed large before me, looking every bit a queen.

Her perfectly coiffed hair was up, a sheer blinding white from root to tip, capped off with an enormous hat sporting what had to be an ostrich plume. She wore a velvet dress and jacket that suited her stature and poise. Her back was ramrod straight, giving her an imperious gaze, and beneath her arm she carried a yappy little dog, as white as her hair.

I had the unaccountable urge to either bow or curtsy, and I wasn't sure which to try. Uncle Fred just removed his hat and said, as convivially as I'd ever heard him speak, "Good morning to you, Madame."

"Good morning, Fred." I was surprised to hear that her voice carried the same midwestern flatness as our own. "I see you've brought an assistant."

"The assistant brought herself," he said, looking down at me. This time I did curtsy, saying the only thing that popped into my head, "Ma'am."

She looked amused. "So it's a girl underneath all that denim."

"Ma'am," I agreed, silently hating myself. Apparently, that was all I was capable of saying at the moment.

"Madame," she corrected. "You will call me Madame."

Then to my uncle, "Bud's already out in the yard with Bonnie, putting her through the paces. You may fetch Gaucho if you like." She smiled in a way that on a lesser woman could have come off as a smirk. "The child may watch if she cares to."

Uncle Fred glanced at me then, and I had the distinct feeling he was wrestling with whether or not to send me home.

"I won't be any trouble, Uncle Fred!" I said quickly. "I'll keep out of your way and won't say anything!" I turned my eyes on to full pleading, and after a moment, he relented.

"Just this once," he said. "We're not making this a regular thing."

I nodded, then followed as he made his way to the pasture. I glanced back toward the Madame, but she'd already gone indoors. I vowed to someday get inside that house. She was the most amazing and mysterious woman I'd ever seen. But who was she? I mean, really?

Six

Bud Thurskow, as it turned out, was a hired man, running a proud-looking mare around the paddock. One of the rumors I'd heard about the Madame was that she used to ride horses in the circus. Maybe my uncle was helping her take care of them? But if that was the case, then why him? Unless he had some kind of special horse-training experience I didn't know about. Bud saw us approach and nodded to Uncle Fred. "Gaucho's in a mood today," he called.

"Wonderful," Uncle Fred moaned. Bud smiled at that. How bad could a horse be that both he and the Madame were pawning the job off onto my uncle? To my surprise, though, we walked straight past the stable areas, back to that field where the ostriches meandered about.

Uncle Fred opened the gate. "No coming in," he said to me. "Ostriches may look silly, but when riled, they can kill a man just by kicking. Most of them are docile and easygoing, but Gaucho . . ." He shuddered a little and then pointed to a lone ostrich standing apart from the flock. "Well, he's another matter."

He removed some tack and rope from the gate. "When I get back here," he instructed me, "I need you to open this gate the minute we're coming through and lock it again right after. Think you can do that?"

For once in my life, I was speechless. Then, with an expression probably most often seen on condemned men taking their last steps to the gallows, Uncle Fred began his slow steady walk to the ostrich.

I didn't know much about the birds at the time, but right off the bat the one thing I did notice was the way my uncle was walking. He didn't run straight up to the bird or stomp toward him or do anything that might startle him. Instead, in that odd loping way of his, he began circling the ostrich slowly. I was immediately reminded of our chickens at home when I saw how the bird reacted. First he ruffled his feathers at Uncle Fred's advance. Then he moved away a pace or two, keeping Uncle Fred in sight at all times. While my uncle uncoiled a length of rope, Gaucho surreptitiously moved away in my direction. The other ostriches stood watching. I wondered if there was any room in those pea brains of theirs to gloat over Gaucho's fate. And then, just like that, a rope was tossed through the air and landed over the bird's head, down his snake-like neck.

Immediately Gaucho took off like a shot. He sped to the east, running as fast as those thick legs could carry him. Uncle Fred, meanwhile, had dug in his feet in an attempt to stop Gaucho's advance, but even a full-grown man's muscles are little match for a determined ostrich with escape on his mind. Yet even as my uncle was pulled forward, I could see him wrapping the rope tightly about his arm. With every tug he was getting closer to the bird, until it seemed like he was going to grab the creature around the neck. Nab the ostrich he did, but what he did next caught me out of the blue. Without warning, Uncle Fred swung his leg up over the bird's back until he was riding him like a pretty pony on a sunny sweet day. Maneuvering Gaucho's head in my direction, I heard Uncle Fred shout, "The gate, Suzy! The gate now!"

I'd been so caught up in the whole affair, I'd plumb forgotten the darned gate. Reeling back, I undid the clasp and swung it open just in time for Uncle Fred and Gaucho to come careening through. I turned to watch them as they sailed on, but suddenly I noticed that the remaining flock of ostriches had seen us and was now headed my way. If one headstrong ostrich looked intimidating, imagine eleven more, in various states of advance. I wasn't feeling so cocky with those steely-eyed feather dusters staring me down.

With a small shriek, I threw the gate closed and fumbled with the latch to secure it. I needn't have worried. Once the gate was shut, the ostriches appeared to believe that it didn't exist anymore. They meandered off, high-stepping it in that way that they do. Toe heel. Toe heel. Toe heel. Like the legs have very little to do with whatever is happening up above. I swear, an ostrich's legs could just walk off, leaving the rest of the body behind, and it wouldn't look any less peculiar than it does when they're attached.

My uncle was slowing down, trying to get Gaucho to go where he wanted in the horse paddock. Bud stood holding the reins of the pretty brown mare while taking some pleasure in watching my uncle try to get the ostrich to come forward. I sidled on up to the fence by Bud.

"Hi," I said.

He looked over his shoulder and nodded. "Hi. You Fred's kid?"

"Nope. I'm a spy."

He didn't turn around this time, but I saw him smile. "A spy?"

"Yep. I'm trying to figure out why he's skipping out on my daddy's farm every morning."

Bud nodded slowly to himself. "That explains a lot," he said, but didn't go on since Uncle Fred was having some difficulties. Somewhere between the field and the paddock he'd started slipping backwards, so that all it took from the bird was a hard right before the man went flying off his back into the mud below. Freed of his passenger, Gaucho attempted a victory lap around the paddock. Bud sighed and handed me the horse's reins.

"This is Bonnie Anne," he said. "She's a good girl. Hold on to her for one second, please." And he made his way toward Gaucho. With a practiced movement, Bud grabbed the rope and whipped it around a fence like a sea-soned pro.

While my uncle brushed off the mud as best as he was able, I glanced over at Bonnie Anne. She kind of looked sickened by the sight before her. Uncle Fred came over with some kind of complicated riding gear and proceeded to attach it to Gaucho's head and back. The bird made a couple feeble attempts to bite, but his aim was not true. When the tack was on well enough, Uncle Fred came over to get the horse.

"So you come over here every morning to ride ostriches?" I asked.

"Not exactly," he said. "You know who Madame Maran- tette is, don't you?"

I nodded. "Sure. Circus lady."

"That's right. She was with Ringling Brothers."

"And she drives the surrey in the parade every county fair." I thought about it. "That's all I know for sure."

"Well, you're right about the surrey," he said. "And the bird who pulls her is Gaucho. She's got a whole field of birds over there, but for some reason she says Gaucho is the stron- gest and the best. And the orneriest," he added, scratching his back for a second. "She's got plans for this next parade. Big ones. And she's letting me lend a hand."

"You?" I scrunched up my nose. "Why you?"

"Why not me?" he countered. "Bud works for her, but no one else round here would do much to help her."

"Whaddaya mean?" Folks loved her in the parades. I tried thinking back to if ever I heard people talking bad about her.

Uncle Fred's face turned a funny color, like a dirty brick. "Don't want to go spreading rumors about a lady," he said under his breath. "I just know what she's told me about her life. People here have other ideas of what all she's gotten up to."

"Like what?"

He glanced over and saw the interest in my eyes. It didn't sit well with him, though, so he switched the subject fast. "I've some experience training horses. I guess you've heard I've had a couple jobs over the years?"

Now it was my turn to be cagey. I didn't think it would do me much good to go telling him what all Daddy and Granny had said about him in the past, so I just cocked my head and waited.

"I lived out west for a time handling cattle and horses. Got pretty good at it. I told that to the Madame when I approached her about working together."

"Why'd you approach her at all?" I asked. "Thought you already had a job with Daddy."

He looked a little sheepish. "Well, now, I'd heard of the Madame before. Knew she'd been with the circus. And . . . something about the possibility of working for her instead of in the fields . . . it would just suit me better, that's all. Besides," he said, as brightly as he was able, "she said she had a project that she needed help with."

"For the parade?" I asked.

He smiled. "After a fashion. Might involve breaking a world record too."

"Who would? You would?"

"Not me. Her."

I gaped at him. "But she's so old!" I frowned over at Gaucho. "She's not gonna . . . ride him, is she?" I briefly tried to picture that statuesque old lady atop that giant bouncy bird.

Uncle Fred did that snort-laugh sound again, like he was thinking the same thing I was. "Not exactly. The Madame's riding days are long past. No. . . ." He looked to the distance. "This is different. You see Gaucho over there?" I nodded. "Well, she has half a mind to train him up not to just pull a surrey by himself, but with Bonnie Anne here alongside."

I blinked. "Come again?"

Slowly, "She wants an ostrich and a horse to pull her, together, in the surrey."

Surreys are funny things. I've always seen a lot of wagons and carriages around the country, but whenever I've seen a surrey, it always looks slightly ridiculous. They're just these miniature carriages for one. That's the kind of thing the Madame rode in at the parade. It was strange enough to see an ostrich doing a horse's job. But working together?

I stared at my uncle like he'd grown two heads.

He threw up his hands. "I know. I know. But she swears it can be done."

"How?"

He sighed. "It all breaks down like this. The horse and the

ostrich have to get along. Their stride, which is to say footstep lengths, have to match. And, finally, they have to move at the same speed." He took off his hat and rubbed his eyes, looking more tired than ever. "I guess this is why I got the job. Nobody else would be so fool as to take it on."

"What about Bud?" I said.

"He's been with her since her days in Europe," he said. "He's a horseman. This ostrich nonsense is all me."

"He seems to know his way around ostriches," I said, nodding my head to where Bud was leading Gaucho around the mud.

Uncle Fred nodded. "If the bird's escaped, there's no one else you'd want to bring it back. But like he put it to me the first day, this is the Madame's pet project, and I'm her pet trainer. He's happy to help out, but I'm the one that's going to have to come up with the solution to getting them to pull at the same time. Trouble is"—he sighed—"I can't stay on that bird more than a minute without flying to the floor."

"Why do you have to ride him?" I asked. "Don't you just have to attach him to the surrey with Bonnie Anne?"

He shook his head. "Remember that part when I said you have to get those two moving at the same rate? Well, a horse you can reason with. Here, look." And he pulled the reins and gently guided Bonnie's head down. "Look into her eye here."

I gave Uncle Fred a suspicious glance, but then looked.

It was a regular old horse's eye. Bonnie Anne snorted a little, but let me look down, down, down inside of it.

"You see that?" my uncle said. "You see how there's someone inside? Someone you can reason with? Horses have souls, Suzy."

"Preacher say that?" I asked, smiling at the man who hadn't been to church since he moved back to town.

He brushed the question off like it was a pesky bee. "Doesn't have to. You know it's true every time you look in their eyes. But an ostrich . . ." He flung a hand at Gaucho and let Bonnie's head go. "Look into the eye of one sometime. Not that one, course. He'll peck off your nose soon as look at you. But try to go down deep into that eye and you know what you'll see?"

I shook my head.

"Absolutely nothing," Uncle Fred said. "It's a shallow pool. No depth to it. Horses may have souls, but ostriches? They do not. No more than giant chickens would."

I had never thought much about the spiritual lives of barnyard beasts, but it seemed to me that even without a soul, Gaucho had more spit and personality than most of the other animals I'd encountered in my days combined. An ornery personality, sure. But a personality.

Uncle Fred looked confused for a moment. "Now, what was I saying? Oh, right. So horses you can reason with to go fast or slow. You can't train an ostrich that way, though. The Madame has some trick where she can get Gaucho to pull her along with verbal commands, but aside from stop and go she can't modulate his speed. That's why they always have her at the head of the parade every year."

I nodded, remembering this to be true.

"So how do you get him to fall in line?" he continued. "The only thing I can figure is that you have to ride him down. Nothing tires an ostrich faster than a human rider. Only I can't stay on more than a minute or two, and Bud's too smart to try."

I thought about this. "No one else on this farm?"

"No one but the Madame and a few farm girls she hires to take care of things." He smiled. "Wouldn't want to see her try either. Apparently, she broke her hip in a throw from a horse a couple years ago and never quite recovered." He turned back to the yard. "All the more reason why we want to get this right. Get it wrong, she gets thrown, and that could be the end of it."

I sighed. "Okay, Uncle Fred. You convinced me. I'll do it."

He turned to me, all confused. "Do what now?"

"I'll do it," I just repeated, then turned to him with a smile. "I'll ride your darned ostrich."

Seven

"I'm lighter."

"Suzy . . ."

"I've been riding animals since before I could walk."

"An ostrich isn't the same as . . ."

"I can grip harder than anyone you've ever met."

I was ticking off the reasons for my very good idea on my fingers, one by one, while Uncle Fred stood before me and began to give in. Mimi says that this is one of my weirder talents. "Most kids, when they want something, just ask for the same thing over and over, like it's going to make a difference," she once said. "But you? You ask for the same thing over and over too—you just do it with different words every time. It's like you're this stingy yellow jacket, pricking the grown-ups in so many different spots that they just give up with you."

I was stinging Uncle Fred pretty hard, and it took some convincing. I don't think he'd have agreed if he hadn't been so desperate for this job. Just why he was desperate remained a mystery to me. Were things so dull back at the farm that he needed some wild ostrich and former circus performer to liven up his days? Truthfully, I didn't really care. Riding an ostrich would be the most exciting thing to ever happen to me in my entire lifetime. Uncle Fred eventually agreed, but with all kinds of rules about how the minute I got even the slightest bit hurt it was over.

It took a little more convincing, actually, to get Bud to agree to it. He didn't like the plan from the start. As far as he was concerned, this was the Madame's madcap idea and that was fine, but getting innocent children trampled by psychotic poultry was not a good idea, no matter how you sliced it. It was only when Uncle Fred swore he'd take full responsibility for my actions, and I bragged that I had the strongest grip in southwest Michigan (which Uncle Fred could back up), that he relented.

It took zero convincing to get the Madame on board. She pretty much heard the plan and nodded. "Good." Then to me, "See that you do it sidesaddle." Then she walked into the house and shut the door.

I stood on the porch gaping like a guppy. Sidesaddle? That old-fashioned way women used to sit where both their legs were on one side of a horse? I knew that in the old days sidesaddle was supposed to be the ladylike way of riding, but for crying out loud this was the twentieth century. She might as well have asked me to put on a hoopskirt and call everyone "thee" and "thou." Heck, I'd never ridden sidesaddle a day of my life. Didn't you need a fancy saddle for it or something?

I turned to Uncle Fred. "Did she just say what I thought she said?"

He blinked slowly, then eyeballed the windows of the house and the paddock keenly. "Can't see the ostrich field as well as the paddock from the house," he said under his breath. I knew what he was saying. He was telling me that if I rode Gaucho in the field, I could do it the regular way, gripping him with my knees, without the Madame seeing. Without a word, I nodded, and our great ostrich experiment began.

Right away we encountered the problem with our plan. In the paddock I could have stood on the wooden fence rail and launched myself onto the bird's back fairly easily. The pasture, however, was surrounded by raw baling wire that no fool would stand on, no matter how thick the soles of her shoes. Uncle Fred mentioned the possibility of him picking me up and launching me onto Gaucho's back, but my silent glare told him that this plan was right out.

It was Bud who provided the answer to our prayers. After hearing us nattering on about it, back and forth, he walked off and returned with a short stepladder. All the better for getting high enough to jump onto an angry ostrich.

Next came figuring out how to get on the bird from the ladder itself. When Gaucho was led from the paddock back to the pasture, he was an intimidating monstrosity. His head didn't bob about at all. Horses' heads bob. Ostriches walk as delicately as my older sister dancing with her boyfriends, but there's a smoothness to the upper half of an ostrich that's at odds with the grotesque thickness of their gangly bottoms. Gaucho glanced over at us, all set to shake off the tack that Bud had so meticulously attached—you could see his little-bitty brain going a mile a minute—when, instead, Bud led him over to the ladder where I was standing.

"Don't move," Bud told me conversationally. "If he doesn't like you, he can strike that beak out with some force. Just stand still and calm. He'll get bored if he doesn't think you're a threat."

So, trying to look as calm as my wildly beating heart would allow, I attempted to resemble something an ostrich would find boring. A rock, perhaps. Or an oddly shaped cloud. And it must have worked, because a couple of seconds later Gaucho was inspecting a particularly tasty-looking grasshopper fluttering on the grass below.

"Now would be a good time," Bud said quietly. The ostrich was pretty close to me, turned so his head was away. Still, I wasn't quite tall enough to just sit straight down on him. Gauging the distance, I decided to do a small jump. I wasn't a big girl. It was possible he wouldn't even notice me, right?

As it turns out, no amount of weight, regardless of girth or lack thereof, is small enough for an ostrich to ignore. The minute my rump hit those feathers, Gaucho was off and running. And, as I had not planned on where my hands would grasp when I hit, I was thrown through the air and landed on my back with a thump in the wild daisies and cornflowers.

Uncle Fred came running over. "Are you all right?" he asked. I could see he was regretting this plan already, so I made a big show of smiling like he'd just offered me a hundred nickels. "Hunky-dory!" I said with a thumbs-up, which might have been pushing it a bit far.

The wind had been knocked right out of me, but it wasn't any worse than falling out of a tree. I shook myself off a little, then headed back to the ladder. Seeing the look on my face, Bud and Uncle Fred cornered the now-flustered Gaucho and brought him back.

On the second attempt, I managed to grab the reins of the bird, but didn't get my leg all the way over. On the third attempt, my legs were on but too far back, so when he ran I just slid backwards, easy as you please. The fourth attempt . . . I'll stop with all the attempts.

To make matters worse, Uncle Fred was getting more and more antsy every time I ended up on the ground. I had to keep him from suddenly calling the whole thing off. So every time I landed in a blasted heap, I'd bounce back up again like some spring-loaded jack-in-the-box. The minute my rear hit the dirt, I'd leap into the air with this big goofy grin on my face. Grown-ups get a lot more relaxed when they think you're having fun. Trouble was, my bottom wasn't made of rubber, and the more it landed in the dirt the less fun it felt. Once or twice I wasn't able to keep the grimace of pain off my face before lapsing back into an easygoing smile or a loud "That was a good one!" Still, I knew that if I didn't come up with a solution to this painful pattern soon, Uncle Fred would declare the whole idea a bad one. It wasn't until the fifteenth attempt (I was keeping track) that I figured out the trick.

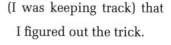

The fourteenth time I'd landed, I'd seen my uncle shake his head and start to cross the field. Before he could, though, it suddenly hit me. I'd been making attempts to hold the reins, but because of my height and the height of Gaucho's head, this wasn't really working for me. On attempt number fifteen,

 I would do something a little more basic. So before Uncle Fred could get to me, I landed, climbed the ladder, ignored the tack, and held on to the bird's neck instead.

If I had taken the time to think about it, I would have assumed Gaucho's neck would feel like the base of a young birch tree, all smooth and bumped. The fact that it was flesh caught me off guard, though I don't know why it should have. It reminded me of the time I'd held a garter snake in my hands, feeling this pulsing and gyrating just under the skin, only hinting at the muscles over muscles over muscles there. Gaucho's neck was like that. All girth and ripples, undulating there beneath the surface.

He also stank like a wet hen.

Gaucho didn't care for any of this, by the way. Didn't care for me sitting there in the first place and especially didn't like little, grippy human fingers on his neck region. He took off like a shot once more, but this time, my hands held on like there was no tomorrow, and around and around we went. When he wasn't trying to outright shake me, he was just careening from place to place. More than once he looked back at me, peeved, but since an ostrich's neck isn't built like an owl's, he was unable to peck me off the way he would have liked. I, meanwhile, just held on tighter and tighter. More than once I felt my knees start to loosen, but my hands weren't gonna give up now. It felt like we were going as fast as my horses at home could gallop, maybe faster. Everything whipped by me at speeds no human legs could match.

Then Gaucho began to slow down. He stumbled, even, and that wasn't something I was ready for. Bud yelled something on the side, but it wasn't making any sense to me.

"You're cutting off his air," he yelled again.

Oh. Ever so slightly I released my grip, and Gaucho began to recover.

"Sorry, boy," I murmured. "I don't want to hurt you any." He didn't act like he heard me, but he didn't speed up either.

"Bring him this way," my uncle called from the other end of the pasture.

Easy for him to say. Without the reins, I didn't have much

of any way to steer, short of grabbing his head and turning it. Fortunately, Bud saw the problem and ran over to take the reins.

It might have been the repeated attempts at his back, the actual running, or the lack of oxygen to his brain, but for the first time, Gaucho came easy. We led him back to the paddock, and I slipped off before we came too close in sight of the house. I would love to tell you that when he was hitched up next to Bonnie, he was as docile as a lamb, but the fact of the matter is that while he wasn't quite as high-strung, he didn't like the idea of being that close to a horse. The two shied away from one another, and by the end of it that fool surrey hadn't moved even so much as an inch.

Bud sized me up as I walked all bow-legged to the fence, and he gave me a nod. "You just kept getting back up" was all he said. It was a statement of fact, not a compliment, but it made me feel like he'd given me a great big bag of praise. "Never saw anything like it."

After it became clear that today would not be a successful surrey day, Uncle Fred said it was time to head back to the farm, what with the sun getting so high and all. We started loping back the way we'd come, me feeling every bruise and fall. It took a full half hour before I heard him chortle.

"Darndest thing I ever saw," he said. "This was definitely easier than the last few days."

"Speak for yourself," I moaned, rubbing my sore spine. I'd be feeling this morning for a time to come.

Uncle Fred laughed, actually laughed out loud, and then picked me up and put me on his shoulders. "Ride something calmer for a change," he said.

And I took care not to grip any part of him for the rest of the walk home.

Eight

After I returned home that first day and got a talking to about my responsibilities to the family, and a switch to the legs from Granny, my mother and father laid out the situation.

I have heard of families where chores do not exist. In the city, they say, you don't have to do much besides shop for food, cook, make your bed, and do the dishes. Here, chores serve as this marvelous invention of the grown-ups that not only gets kids to do all the work but also keeps kids from ever complaining that they're bored. To skip a chore is akin, in my parents' minds, to setting the house on fire. Unthinkable.

First up, I had to do my regular chores. Milking and egg collecting and feeding the chickens were already done for the day, since my siblings had had to pick up my slack (they were giving me the stink eye for the better part of the day, thanks to that). That meant I was on dish and laundry duty. Added to that for punishment was beating the rugs (which I kind of secretly enjoy, but don't tell anyone); dusting the parlor; mucking out the stall of our old horse, Frances; and cleaning the truly disgusting chicken coop.

My parents relayed all this to me and I took it. "Yes, ma'am. Yes, sir." No sass. No protestations. You'd have thought I was the most sorrowful critter that ever crossed them.

It was all part of my cunning plan.

Sitting there on Uncle Fred's shoulders on the way home, I'd come to the realization that in spite of his saying, "We're not making this a regular thing," we were, in fact, making this a regular thing. I didn't fall off that ostrich over and over so that I could someday tell a funny story to my grandkids. I fell off that ostrich over and over so that I could fall off it over and over again tomorrow, and the day after that, and the day after that.

There wasn't a lot about me that distinguished me from other farm girls out there in this great nation of ours, but there was one thing. I got to ride an ostrich. And there was no way I was letting go of that. Instinctively, I clenched my fists.

Of course, if Mama and Daddy decided to give me an outright "never again" on the matter, then I'd be stuck. Uncle Fred would refuse to take me along, and no amount of sneaking over there would change his mind. That meant I had to do something I really hated. I had to simultaneously become the Sorrowful Repentant Child and the Perfect Daughter to get what I wanted.

And what I wanted was weird.

So here I was, nodding my head, willing a golden halo to float down from heaven and plant itself upon my brow. Mama always looks like she's cutting off one of her digits whenever she punishes her children. Daddy's more at home as a disciplinarian, but you never get the sense he enjoys it. So if it had been just the two of them in the room, my job would have been easier. Only problem was, there was a third party involved. Sitting there. In a rocking chair. Knitting a baby bootie for little Catalonia.

Granny. The true obstacle to success.

Sometimes Bill would say to me accusingly that Granny liked me better than my siblings. This was not true. If anything, I bugged the living daylights out of Granny because I gave her so few reasons to yell at me. So with me skipping out on the chores, she wasn't about to miss the rare opportunity of watching me endure punishment. My legs still stung from where her switch had caught me unawares when I'd gotten back in the house.

It was time to make my move. But first I needed to get Granny out of my way. She couldn't tell Mama and Daddy what to do, but she did have some kind of influence over them that I couldn't beat. Time for a distraction.

"Mama? Daddy?" My eyes started to fill up, and I made my bottom lip quiver with the tiniest of motions. So small that you might not actually see it, just sense the vibrations in the air. "May I use the privy and then come right back?" The clear implication being that I was gonna bawl my eyes out there and then settle in for more browbeating.

Mama looked half like she wanted to cry herself. "Be quick about it," she said.

Oh, I would. Like a jackrabbit I nipped out of there and beelined for the great outdoors. Not for the privy, though. Instead I swung a right and headed for the orchards, where I knew I could find her. Dotty. My little sister.

My savior.

Sure as shooting she was sitting there beneath some dirty old crab apple tree playing with her corn husk dolls. Dotty owned an army of them. Eighty at least. Any time we had

corn for dinner there she'd be, plowing through the discards
so she could turn more of them into tiny friends. Under that
tree she'd made several corn husk cities, and she appeared to
be setting up some kind of corn husk parade route between
them. She'd been spending a lot of time here since Mama had
little Catalonia in her life. I didn't think Mama ever wanted
another baby, but something in her woke up every time she
looked at Aunt Juliet's child. When Dotty wasn't moaning for

Mama's attention, she usually retired here, where at least she had the undivided attention of her very own handmade civilization.

I felt a little pang of sympathy as I approached. It wasn't that Dotty and I didn't get along; we just had too many years between us and too few interests. I did not list corn husk dolls on my roster of Fun Things to Do.

"Hi, Dotty," I said as I approached. She barely glanced up at me, then back down to what she was doing.

Uh-oh. I knew that look. She was in the throes of some kind of storyline. Might be hard to shake her from it.

"Uh, Dotty?" No response. "I need a favor."

She looked up a little longer now. Then held up one of the dolls. "Wanna play?"

"I can't," I said. "I'm in trouble with Mama and Daddy."

She squinted her eyes and looked kind of confused. "'Cause you skipped all your chores today?"

"Yep."

"I can't do your chores," Dotty pointed out logically.

"No, it's not that kind of favor. Look, I need you to get Granny out of the room with them."

Dotty has many distinctive qualities, but one of the things I admire the most, only second to her ability to sleep like the dead, is her complete and utter lack of fear around Granny. It literally makes no sense. I've been scared of Granny since before I knew how to talk, but when Dotty was born, somehow she got it into her head that Granny was a nice old lady, and she's never lost that certainty. Even so, she wasn't looking at me with any smiles.

"How'm I gonna do that?"

"Tell her . . ." I glanced about frantically. Outhouse tears are only allowed if they are brief outhouse tears. "Tell her you want her to see your parade route."

Dotty considered my words, so I followed them up with, "And if you do, then I'll play with you every night after supper. For one week."

Her eyes lit up. I never played with Dotty, always tossing off some excuse to go do other things on the farm. I felt a little bad about that. Even Bill played with Dotty more than I did, running around with her on his back like he was a mad bronco and her a wild cowboy trying to break him. I probably could have gotten her to do anything in the world if I offered to play with her willingly. In any case, the deal was done.

I made a run for the kitchen and found the scraps bin, where the remains of breakfast were sitting. Mama had served eggs with onions this morning, and after the careful application of some onion peels to the eyes, I stumbled back into the room where Mama, Daddy, and Granny were consulting, looking for all the world a little worse for the wear. Mama made a swift movement, as if to scoop me into her arms, but stopped herself.

I looked both my parents in their eyes. I couldn't overdo this or they'd know I wasn't being sincere.

"Mama. Daddy. I'm sorry I didn't do my chores. It will not happen again, I promise. And I'll do all the extra ones too, just like you said."

They looked relieved to hear it, and even Granny made a little conciliatory "Hrmph" sound from her chair.

"But I want to ask something too. If that's okay." I could see Granny sitting up a little straighter in her chair. Like a lion that smells blood way off across the savanna. I was stepping out of Sorrowful Repentant Child territory into Child Asking for Favors territory, and she was gonna personally sound the death knell on anything I asked, no matter what it was. If I asked to blink, she'd say no. I could see Mama cut her a glance, aware of what was going to happen but powerless to overrule her mother-in-law. Daddy shifted in his seat.

Fortunately, my words were Dotty's cue. She bounded into the room without looking at anyone else and headed straight for Granny. "Come on, Granny! I wanna show you my parade!" She took hold of one of the woman's hands and tugged.

Bill's wrong. Granny only has one favorite in the family and it ain't me. She's never been able to deny Dotty anything, not a day of her life, but now she was in a right pickle. She loved Dotty but loved seeing me punished too. "Granny, please!" Dotty begged.

"Now, you're just gonna have to wait a few moments here, sweetheart," Granny tried, but Mama, relieved, said, "Oh, don't you worry, Mother. I think we've got a handle on Suzy ourselves. Dotty, why don't you show Granny what you made." And like a little weight lifter, Dotty single-handedly pulled our grandmother from the room. I felt everyone around me exhale when it happened. Like we'd all been holding our breaths until that exact moment in time.

"I'm sorry, what were you gonna say, sweetheart?" Daddy said to me.

I looked him square in the eye. "I am sorry for what I did. But I wondered . . . if I keep doing all these chores, not just today but every day, would it be okay if I went with Uncle Fred again?"

This was not what they'd expected. They'd chalked up my running off this morning to a child's natural curiosity. That's how Fred had sold it to them anyway.

"Again?" Mama looked positively befuddled and Daddy was equally confused. I could see that their instincts were to say no, but instead of plowing forward with some kind of fast-talking, I just slowed myself way down.

"Well . . ." I smiled a little. "I liked looking at the ostriches. And Fred let me help out with some of the chores over at the Madame's. She's old and can't do a lot of stuff like she used to. I thought maybe I could help her some." Pause. "I don't think a lot of people visit her much. I don't think she gets a lot of help."

The way I put it sounded like I was making some sweet old lady tea in bed. Plus, I was banking on what Fred had told me about there not being a lot of people coming round there. I was being a saintly child helping out an elderly neighbor. If Granny had been in the room, she'd have seen right through me in a hot minute. Instead, she was crouched down in the orchard, probably watching an endless procession of corn husk couples traipse through their tiny town.

"Oh!" Mama glanced over at Daddy, who wasn't smiling but wasn't arguing either. "Well, if it's to help out a neighbor . . . What do you think, dear?"

Daddy chewed it over for a minute. "Let me talk to Fred," Daddy said eventually. "Apparently, she's paying him for whatever it is he's doing, and that's money coming back to this farm. So if he thinks you won't be in the way . . ." He shrugged. "Don't see why not. BUT," he added, seeing my growing look of delight, "you were the one who offered double the chores. You stick to that agreement."

"I will!" I said eagerly. Secretly, I hoped Mama would

reduce those chores on the sly, on account of me being such a good daughter.

"All right, then," he said. "I'm sure you still have chores to do. Go on." And I was dismissed.

I managed to keep from dancing out of the room, but it was a near thing.

Nine

As it later turned out, that spying mission I'd worked so very hard on was pretty much rendered moot a day or two later. If I'd just had some patience, I would have heard about Uncle Fred's extracurricular activities from the other folks in Burr Oak. Seems a man can't hightail it to an ex–circus performer's house on the sly all that easily in this neck of the woods. Word of him spread like wildfire in a place where truly interesting gossip only flies by once in a blue moon. Folks started calling Uncle Fred "Ostrich Man" behind his back, though they could have called him that right up to his face and I doubt he would have cared.

Interestingly, the gossip never seemed to name me much

at all, except perhaps to suggest that I too was skipping out on my farm chores to play along at Uncle Fred's game. I wish that had been the case.

It didn't take me long to figure out that the only way I was going to survive the oncoming avalanche of work was to get organized. So I put a system in place. If I made certain to do some of my chores the night before, and the other unavoidable ones (like collecting eggs) before I took off with Uncle Fred, then I still didn't have much time to myself in the afternoon thanks to the dramatic storylines involving Dotty's corn husk kingdom (not to mention the *rest* of my chores), but it was doable. Granny, in case you had any doubts, did NOT approve. She'd huff at me when I'd return each day, but she couldn't override the deal I'd struck with Mama and Daddy (and, after a fashion, Dotty). My siblings didn't care much either, just so long as they didn't get stuck with my jobs on top of their own. Uncle Fred, for his part, seemed happy to have me along. He never said as much, but I noticed he'd always smile when he saw me approach him on the path in the morning, and that made his face seem a little less hangdog than before.

As it turned out, ostrich riding was tough, but I was getting the hang of hanging on. The first few times, I clung to Gaucho's neck, for sure, but after a while I managed to use the reins. It turned out to be a little bit easier when I did that. Gaucho would swerve off back the way *he* wanted until you kept him going in the direction *you* wanted, but he was more manageable the more I rode him. Bud said at some point he'd begin to recognize me. Ostriches can't smell very well, so they rely almost entirely on their eyesight. I wondered if Gaucho would ever have a name for me. If he did, it would probably be something pretty basic, like Loud Small Person.

I liked the idea of Gaucho recognizing me, so I asked Bud one day, "Can ostriches hear?"

"Dunno. Can any birds hear?" he replied.

"Well . . ." I felt stupid but plowed on. "I don't see any ears on him."

Bud always said that I asked him my most complicated questions when he was in the middle of doing something that required his full concentration. Right now he was getting the surrey attached to Bonnie Anne, so with more than a bit of exasperation he said, "He can hear. Why? Do you want to talk to him?"

"Yep. I want him to remember my voice," I said.

He smiled. "You can try it. Just don't expect him to talk back much. Even if he could talk, I don't think he'd say anything you'd want to hear." Pause. "Probably a lot of cursing. What with you squeezing all the air out of him."

I rolled my eyes but decided to give it a try. On a day

when Uncle Fred was willing for me to try something new, I put the plan into action.

Talking to the ostrich was going to be my primary job today. And yet, I quickly figured out that while talking to a dog or a cat or even a horse is easy, talking to a large violent bird doesn't come quite as naturally.

"Um. Good morning, Gaucho," I said that first day. I felt weirdly awkward. I glanced over at Uncle Fred, who gave me a thumbs-up.

Pause. "Nice weather we're having?"

Since an ostrich's eyes are on the sides of its head, sometimes it's a little hard figuring out if it's looking at you. It was not hard figuring out if Gaucho was looking at me right now, though, since he was making a point of showing that he definitely was not. It was as if he was thinking hopefully, "Child? What child? There is no child here."

Okay, enough of that. I took his reins and led him to the ladder, where I clambered up. I had decided that it would be a good idea to start by saying the same thing every time I got onto him. That way, he'd know what to expect. My choice of words?

"Up, up, Gaucho!" I cried it loudly, then launched myself onto his back.

The ostrich could not have cared less about what I was

saying. He still didn't love the small human on his back, but sometimes when I got up there, it was as if he was slowly coming around to the idea.

Not this time. This time he started into a run, and so I tried to calm him down with sweet nothings while also holding on tight.

"Good, Gaucho. Sweet, Gaucho. You're such a pretty bird. Such a nice pretty bird."

No change in his speed. I tried a different tactic.

"Boy, you sure do run fast. Why don't you run slower? Or, I don't know, less bumpy? Less bumpy would be good. Want to give it a try?"

He did not want to give it a try, and he indicated this by swerving sharply several times in the hopes of dislodging me for good.

Sweet nothings yielded nothing. Suggestions were useless. I tried threats.

"Do you know what feather dusters are made of? Ostriches. I bet you'd make five hundred good feather dusters easily. Is that what you want? Ow! Is it?"

The "Ow" was in reaction to Gaucho's realization that if he scraped alongside the fence, he could get me to shift my weight in such a way where it might be easier to bump me off. That meant the rest of our conversations sounded like this:

"Gaucho, don't you dare get near the fence."

Bump.

"I'm serious. Ow! Stop trying to rub me off."

Bump.

"You nutty bird, cut it out!"

Bump.

Gaucho couldn't talk, but his actions spoke louder than words. When we were done and Uncle Fred had gotten the reins in hand, I slid off onto the ladder and climbed down slowly.

"How'd it go?" he asked with a smile.

"I think I'm more tired talking and riding him than just riding him," I huffed. I turned back to glare at the animal. He didn't even have the good grace to look tuckered. I switched my glare to Uncle Fred instead. "You think he'll ever get used to me?"

"He ought to. Only, if you keep screaming at him, he may not be able to tell the difference between you and a teeny-tiny screech owl. Might get the two of you mixed up."

I stood, amazed. A joke! An honest-to-goodness joke from my dour uncle! I was so shocked I actually grinned back at him, even as I started plucking the splinters out of the legs of my overalls. A flash of something out of the corner of my eye distracted me, though, and I saw the Madame turn heel back to her home.

I watched her close the door behind herself. Of course, riding the bird was all well and good, but it was rapidly becoming secondary to what I really wanted to do: find out more about the Madame. From the moment I'd laid eyes on her, I felt something that went beyond just being curious. It wasn't that she was rich or anything. We had plenty of rich female types in town, with their ladies' societies and readings and whatnot. Nothing duller than a soft brain with money, my granny liked to say.

It wasn't that the Madame was famous either. Famous is neat, but you could be famous for bad things easy as good. My great-uncle Artie, for example, was famous in my family for getting his little toe cut off when his brother was splitting wood. Artie kept sticking it under the axe and then taking it away to be a goof. His brother warned him to quit it, since he wouldn't be able to stop the axe if Artie was too slow. Artie slowed down, the axe fell, and there you go. Famous Artie, the four-toed.

No, the thing about the Madame was that she'd clearly done the one thing I yearned to do. She'd seen the whole wide world. I mean, circus performers don't stay in one spot. They have to travel. Sure, she'd chosen to plant herself in the one place where I already was, but that was her choice. I wanted that choice. I wanted to be able to decide where I was or wasn't any given day. Particularly if the "where I wasn't" was here.

The last thing I expected, then, was for my granny to give me the goods on where the Madame came from. Funny that the person most dead set on keeping me around was the one who set my brain aflame.

I was in the kitchen helping Granny, Mama, and Aunt Juliet make apple pies. Uncle Fred was off actually working the farmland that morning, so I was stuck doing useful chores around the house. Aunt Juliet was making crusts with Mama, which she did without enthusiasm. I was on apple-peeling duty, which sounds easy, but I am not a born apple peeler. Basically, I just sorta chip off the peel as I go. Mama could take even the dullest knife, pick up an apple, and with deft movements make a long, looping, single strand o' peel. But she never says boo when I chip away at the fruit, even though more apple probably ends up on the counter than in the pie.

Granny, on the other hand, has a tendency to injure herself in the kitchen. I get the feeling she has as much patience for the rigmarole of cooking as I do. She is fast and stubborn and crotchety. This time she'd sliced her finger and the dang thing was dripping blood absolutely everywhere. She tried to grab for another apple to slice it when Mama grasped her by the wrist and said, "Mother! Stop that right now and put something on that wound. You're gonna bleed to death!"

"Ain't got enough blood to bleed to death," Granny

snarled back, but she let Mama lead her to a chair in the dining room to sit for a spell.

"Suzy, go get your granny some cheesecloth to bind herself
up with before she turns us all cannibal with her drippings."

I raced around till I found it, and next thing I knew I was
binding her up myself.

"Tighter," Granny said to me.
"Gotta cut off the blood flow."

"Won't that hurt you?" I
asked. Granny just responded
with a snort. To her
mind, pain wasn't

something a real woman took into consideration. She bore every scar and bruise with pride and urged the rest of us to do the same.

As I started reworking the cloth, she fixed her steely eyes right on me. "You been going to old Emma Peek's house the last few days, is that it?"

I frowned and lost my concentration on the gauze, so I had to start again. "Who?"

"Emma Peek. Oh, I'm sorry." She got all sarcastic on me then. "*Madame* Marantette's what she's going by now, is it? Got you bowing and scraping to her, no doubt, when all she's ever been is one of the plain old Peek girls from up a ways."

I stopped what I was doing and looked up in shock. "You mean she's from around here?"

Granny snorted. "Around here? Child, she's Mendon born and raised. Started out racing her daddy's horses when she was younger. Always was a weird one. She and that sister of hers, going riding when there was real work to do. We all reckoned she'd never find a man at that rate, and then what do you figure?" A snarl curled at the corner of her lip. "She married one of the Marantette boys. Catholic kids, and her Methodist, pure and simple. No one approved of that one. Time was, they owned the most farmland in town." She peered down at me. "What? You thought the Marantette Farms all east of here belonged to *her*?"

I hadn't given much thought to who owned what. I sat there, soaking this all in. "Did her husband die on her?"

"Die? Die! Ha!" She cackled at the thought. "No, but she shamed him good and hard. When the Marantette family said to have the marriage annulled, she went along with it. Only she took something from them as part of the deal. Something they'd live to regret when she went off and got all fancy on us."

"What?"

Granny leaned in close so that I could smell that one rotten tooth she had clear in the back of her mouth, and the spearmint she'd chomp to cover it up. "The name."

"The name?"

"Took their fool name, didn't she? Goodbye, Emma Peek! Hello, *Madame* Marantette." Granny shook her head at that one, and in the middle of it I could see just the faintest glimmer of admiration. "Stole something from those rich folks they couldn't steal back. Darndest thing."

"Then what?"

"Then?" The admiration sizzled out of her like butter on a hot griddle. "Then she got out of town. Had to. No one wanted a formerly married woman around after that, not even her sister. Shamed the Peek family right hard. Dunno if they ever got over it. So while they're trying to live down what she did, she's off doing who knows what." She sucked her teeth.

"Next thing you know they're saying she'd gone to the circus or some such. We heard bits and pieces, but was she here when her father or her mother or even her sister died? Did she come to their funerals? She did not."

"Her sister died?" I asked softly.

All at once Granny came to, suddenly furious at herself for talking. "Now, you call that a bandage? Gimme that thing." Quick as a wink she wrapped up her finger and launched herself from her chair. "Got pies to make. No more stories outta you or I'll give you a much worse job." Never mind that she'd been the one spreading tales.

I couldn't stop thinking about Emma Peek. A farm girl like me. But somehow she went out and became a fancy lady of the world.

I walked into the kitchen and absently picked up another apple to butcher.

The feeling I would get when looking at the tiny map beneath my bed came upon me all at once. If Emma Peek got out and saw the world, there had to be a trick to it. There had to be a secret. I, Suzy Bowles, was getting out of Burr Oak, Michigan.

And the Madame was my ticket out.

Ten

Children aren't allowed in the parlor. That's the fancy room where the grown-ups meet other grown-up guests and talk about the weather and politics and hog prices and that sort of stuff. I am never allowed in the parlor at home, except on fancy Christmasy occasions. Standing in the Madame's parlor was intimidating to say the least. For one thing, she didn't treat me like a child at all. She treated me like an adult, and it was a hard thing to get used to.

When Uncle Fred and I had arrived that morning, I'd done my Gaucho business as usual. Only this time I'd decided that music might work better than talking had, so I tried singing him all the best songs I knew. I went through

"A Bicycle Built for Two" and "Oh My Darling, Clementine" and "Battle Hymn of the Republic." When those didn't seem to make any difference, I switched to Christmas songs like "Jingle Bells," but it felt peculiar belting that song out in the summer. Gaucho just wasn't reacting to anything I was doing anyway, so I gave it one more go and tried out a hymn. THAT got a reaction! About the time I got to the second verse of "Amazing Grace," he was shimmying and turning so hard that the upper half of my body was on the bird and my legs were airborne. Clearly the bird didn't know a fantastic singing voice when he heard one. Never mind Uncle Fred asking why I kept making "screechy sounds" the whole time.

Afterwards, instead of hanging around to watch Gaucho get attached with Bonnie Anne, I silently slipped away and went on up to the house. I didn't want Uncle Fred to know what I was up to. That morning on our walk I'd gotten him to tell me a little more about his cowboy days out west. He told me all kinds of wild stories about the men he'd met out there and what a sky looked like when the horizon wasn't all broken up by trees.

"Just sky, Suzy. Just loads and loads of sky, there for the looking at. Nobody to tell you it's wrong to stare at it a spell." He looked up into our own sky, smiling, but it seemed to remind him of something that brought him back down to earth. "But when I married your aunt Juliet, it wasn't the life for a man with a wife and child. I didn't know anything about kids, but I knew my own would probably need something a little less hectic. Maybe near family." He glanced over at me. "And seeing how you're turning out here . . . well, it just shows I was right, doesn't it?" That last part had a little bit of a pleading quality to it, like he needed me to agree with him, so I nodded my head vigorously and he looked relieved.

I flattered myself that he was getting to like me as much as I was getting to like him, but I knew that he was a grown-up and he'd probably get all funny when I told him I had plans to talk to the Madame myself. So when the coast was clear (which is to say, when Gaucho got ahold of the bull-whip that hung on the side of the paddock gate and attempted to swallow it like spaghetti) I took that as my cue to escape.

The Madame herself answered the door. On occasion, she'd come down to the paddock to watch our progress with Gaucho and Bonnie Anne, but she never stayed very long. I wondered today if she'd been watching us the whole time. A sudden shamefacedness came over me, but before I could beg off, the Madame smiled.

"Miss Suzy," she said. "Delighted to see you. We're overdue for a talk. We'll have tea."

She led me to the parlor, where the interior gloom contrasted sharply with the brightness of the day outside, and then excused herself for a moment. The parlor itself was a seemingly windowless room, lit by a single oil lamp. It was only when I spent some time there that I realized that what looked like part of the walls were in fact heavy curtains, covering windows and keeping out every scrap of sunlight that might dare to fade the fancy furniture inside. I breathed in deep and got a noseful of thick dust. When a room's been alive too long, it sometimes has a tendency to smell like the inside of an old man's jacket pocket. This one sure did anyway.

I spotted a photo album, open on a table. The house was silent as a tomb, so I tiptoed over, keeping one ear cocked toward the hall, and turned the album's pages. There was the Madame with a mustachioed man. There she was on the deck of a train car with "Ringling Brothers Circus" painted bold to one side. The car she was standing in sported the name "ST. PATRICK" on it. "Must be a big fan of the holiday," I muttered to myself. On another page a newspaper article displayed the photograph of a fancy gentleman clasping her hand. Who was he? I read the caption on the photo. "Circus royalty meets the real thing when Madame Marantette kisses the king of England."

My jaw dropped so low I'm surprised it didn't fall into the album.

Suddenly I noticed something. I flipped back through the pages just to make sure.

In each photograph of the Madame, whether she was young or old, she wore a strange silvery-looking brooch. It was hard to make it out in the early photographs, but as time passed I began to see it clearer. It was in the shape of a rider on a horse. A female rider, sitting straight-backed and sidesaddle, wearing an old-fashioned dress with puffed sleeves.

In another photo, the Madame stood next to the mustachioed man along with a gangly, sullen-looking teenage boy and a wistful-looking girl, not a year or two younger than me. I lingered on the photo, then heard the approach of footsteps. Quickly I slammed the book shut (forgetting that it had been open when I'd come in) and ran to the other side of the room.

The Madame returned with a kitchen maid at her side. She indicated a chair of exquisite embroidery, and I tried to surreptitiously check my bottom for dirt as I sat. When was the last time I'd washed these overalls? I prayed nothing disgusting would remain on this chair after I'd vacated it.

Tea was poured ceremoniously for two, and while I blew in my cup, I looked up and froze. To my amazement the Madame was wearing the very brooch that I'd seen in all the photographs. When she glanced over at me, I lowered my eyes, flustered as she spoke.

"You recall my advice to you when you first told me that you would be riding Gaucho for your uncle."

"Advice?" I shrank a little in my seat. "You mean, about riding sidesaddle?"

She blew on her tea and didn't say a word. Just flicked her sharp eyes to meet my own. I squirmed like a toddler and tried a weak protest.

"If I don't get my legs around the body, though, then there's nothing to grip with my knees."

"Pfui!" The Madame made a disgusted sound. "A true rider doesn't use her *knees* to maintain balance on a steed. Your power is in your grasp and poise, not the contortions of your lower extremities."

"Yes, ma'am," I said meekly. She regarded me in silence for a while. Then she raised one long forefinger to tap at her brooch.

"You were looking at this brooch earlier. I could tell. Does it interest you?"

"Yes," I said simply. Simple answers are good. You can only mess up so much when you keep things simple.

"It was a gift from an admirer long, long ago," she said with a smile. "In fact, it is an image of me on a horse. No one could imagine a rider going quite as fast as I could while sitting sidesaddle. I wear it to remind myself and others who I am and what I am capable of. Now, we meet today, Suzy Bowles, to determine what you are capable of."

Her eyes continued to size me up as she took a sip.

"We will start with the overalls. They are suitable for these early days when you are first learning Gaucho's ways. But in time he will grow accustomed to you, and they will no longer be up to the job. When you ride him in the future, it will be in your best dress. Sidesaddle," she repeated. She picked up a tiny sandwich and took a nibble.

Suddenly a whole mess of words burst out of me before I even realized I was going to say them.

"Madame, can I say something? I mean, there's nothing wrong with looking like a farm girl if I'm doing farm chores like riding Gaucho."

The Madame froze, her sandwich dangling precariously between her fingertips, and pinned me to my seat with a look.

"Farm chores?" The words crackled like ice. "Am I to understand you rank riding my ostrich right up there with mucking out the cow stalls?"

"No, ma'am! I mean Madame!" I corrected, suddenly aware that the floor beneath me was starting to give way.

"Farm chores." She pursed her lips in disgust. "There is nothing farm-like to this endeavor, little girl. I am not offering you a mere chore. Let me ask you this: What is the one thing in life that determines your success?"

After a minute, I said, "A rich daddy?" I thought better of it. "Granddaddy?"

She laughed at that. A pure, full-blown laugh that showed

her teeth right back to her molars. They were uncommonly straight. "Perhaps," she said a moment later when she'd recovered herself. "But beyond that."

I shook my head, uncertain.

"Pure dogged tenacity," she said. Then, seeing that I didn't understand, "Bullheadedness. Stubbornness. The inability to give up even when others tell you that you should. In this life, you get ahead if you have brains, and you get ahead if you have beauty. But if you have no more brains and no more beauty than anyone else around you, then you hold on to what you want and you do not let go. No matter how much they try to tell you to abandon all hope. Do you understand?"

She was looking deep into my eyes now, and though I didn't understand, I nodded slowly. She pulled back, looking satisfied.

"This is why I tell you to wear the dress and ride sidesaddle. An ordinary farm girl riding an ostrich is a novelty. A young lady filled with poise and elegance riding an ostrich is an *event*. There is great strength in female confidence. Man is born with muscle, and muscles take no brains. Woman is born with a womb, but creating and sustaining life doesn't require much in the way of brains either. The delicacies of womanhood are, in fact, our strengths. To knit is to clothe.

To embroider is to create. And to ride sidesaddle is more difficult than riding as a man. A man grasps. Anyone may grasp. You and I, we shall ride. And now," she said, glancing at the clock on the mantelpiece, "this is about the time you and your uncle start heading home."

I sat there for a few seconds before I realized I'd just been handed a dismissal. My brain was trying to wrangle with everything she'd just said. What was that about a womb? But the Madame was staring at me pointedly by now, so I awkwardly slid off of the chair, gave a weird little curtsy (I was so befuddled I'm lucky I didn't sink to the floor halfway down), and walked to the front door in a daze.

As she led me to the porch, the Madame said to me, "Allow me to give you a bit of advice with Gaucho. You have ridden him enough to realize that he has a mind of his own. An admirable quality in a human and a potentially bothersome one in a bird. The sole way to master him, beyond merely talking to him"—and here she gave me a significant look—"is to be firm. When dealing with hard-to-handle horses, I am unafraid to stop. I speak to them so that there is no doubt who is in charge, and when I begin again, I am mistress of the day."

"But Gaucho's an ostrich," I said.

"True." She winced. "An ostrich is not a true steed. You cannot truly ride something that refuses to acknowledge itself as a mount. You as much ride an ostrich as you do a snowball plunging down a hill. Yet I have always suspected that there is more to that particular bird than meets the eye. If connections can be made between the brains and intentions of humans and horses, then surely, and at the very least, sense can be taught to an ostrich." Then she smiled. "You remind me a bit of myself when I was young."

I beamed.

"Uncultured. Ignorant in the ways of the world."

I stopped beaming.

"Now then," she said, putting up a hand, "it all worked out for me in the end. Sometimes I think ignorance is what allows us to bash through barriers that we didn't even know existed." She pointed a long finger at me. "Do not overthink your worth."

"Whatever that means, I won't!" I agreed with gusto, figuring honesty was the best way to go here.

She chuckled.

"We will make these teas weekly, and I shall teach you far more than the simple basics. There will be the usual finishing school topics, but also more esoteric knowledge. Information you will not be able to use for years. And you, as payment for these lessons in comportment, will help with my ostrich. What do you think?"

I had no idea what the words "esoteric" or "comportment" or "finishing school" meant. "Comportment" sounded like "compartment." Like she wanted to box me up and ship me somewhere. Which, come to think of it, was kinda what I wanted too. So I looked her in the eye, stuck out one dirty hand for a shake, and smiled.

"When do we start?"

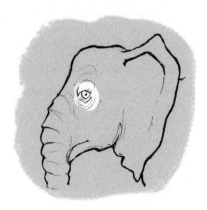

ELeven

Turned out, "comportment" meant "manners." Manners and lessons on how to be a fine lady. That wasn't what I signed up for, but we'd shaken on it (followed by an extended period of the Madame cleaning that same hand with a perfumed handkerchief for so long that I think she was trying to make some kind of a point). There was at least one good thing about these lessons (which tended to include a lot of "Let's correct Suzy on her grammar, posture, poise, eating habits, nose picking, armpit scratching," etc.). When I was in that gloomy parlor room every Monday with the Madame, I didn't think about that louse-riddled puzzle waiting outside.

Gaucho. That big-eyed blunder of a bird. The Madame

was right: Talking alone didn't make any difference to him. You had to do it in a way that told him to pay attention. So every time I said, "Up, up, Gaucho!" I made sure to do it with this extra little yelp in my voice. Maybe someday he'd have to pick my voice out over the voices of a crowd, so the more I did it, the more he'd recognize it. Now, I can't say there was this lightbulb moment where he started recognizing who I was (he probably thought I was a different Loud Small Person every time), but little things started to change. He wasn't trying to rub me off onto the fence anymore. When I got on, he still didn't like it, but he didn't do that shuffling, jumping dance he used to do to dislodge me. And when he ran full out with me on his back, it was something. I know ostriches can't fly, but I swear that bird just soared. He was even pulling alongside Bonnie Anne a little better than before, but half the time he'd stop cold, dead in his tracks, and refuse to budge for man or beast.

It was Uncle Fred who had the idea of what to do about Gaucho.

After I rode the bird around one day, Uncle Fred met us at the gate with an empty feed sack in his hand. Soon as we rode into the paddock, he popped that bag on top of Gaucho's head like an oversized nightcap. The effect was immediate. My formerly rambunctious rambler slowed to a dazed halt. When led, he walked. And when I hopped onto the fence and

Gaucho was saddled up right next to Bonnie Anne, he didn't shy away. She too seemed less perturbed by the bird when she didn't have to look him in the eye. And while getting the two to canter together smoothly was still a ways away, Gaucho seemed content to walk forward, even though he clearly had no idea where he was going. Uncle Fred and I counted that as a victory right there. Even the Madame was impressed, and she commended Uncle Fred's smart thinking when we showed her the results.

On the way home that day, Uncle Fred asked me if I had any interest in celebrating by sharing in some toffee he'd brought along for just this very occasion. The toffee was warm, on account of having been sitting in his pocket for a while, but I took half, and we sat in a nearby meadow, chomping away, staring up at the sky.

After a moment of chewing on it, I figured I needed to ask him something that had been chewing on me.

"Uncle Fred," I asked tentatively. "Why did you ask the Madame to hire you in the first place?"

He didn't answer for a while, and I wondered if he was even going to respond to my question. Then, almost as if he hadn't heard me, he started in on a story.

"I grew up in Burr Oak, same as you. Same as my mama, your granny. Same as her parents before her. When you grow up in a farming family, that's what you do with your life. You farm like your ancestors did, and you don't think much about doing anything else. It's easier that way," he said slowly. "There's so many things that are hard about living that knowing what you're going to do with the rest of your life is at least one less thing to worry about. But for me, it was the opposite. It was a worry because it wasn't what I wanted to do."

"Well, what did you want to do, then?"

He smiled, that strange sad smile of his. "I wanted to run away to join the circus."

"Really?"

"Really," he said. "They travel about a lot. You ever see them come to this part of the state?"

"Once," I said, remembering. "But I was really little then, like four or something. I don't remember much except seeing them riding all about on horses and there being lions, I think?"

"And elephants," he added. "When I was a boy, that was the most exciting thing for me. I'd see these massive creatures, bigger than horses, bigger, it sometimes seemed, than houses. And I just knew I wanted to work with them. Remember when I said looking into the eye of an ostrich is like looking into a shallow pool?"

I nodded.

"Well, looking into the eye of an elephant's the opposite of that. I should know. One night, when the circus came to

town, our whole family headed back home, but I stayed behind. Couldn't have been more than sixteen years of age. It
was pretty clear at that point that I'd be farming if I didn't find
something else to do with myself. Your daddy was eldest, so
he was set to inherit, but they always figured I'd get a pocket
of land of my own nearby too. I figured different. Anyway,
after the show, I found where they kept the elephants, and
moving in the shadows, I was able to come up right to them in

their tent. At first they startled a little, but I think they could tell this skinny little human didn't mean them no harm. I got right up next to this one elephant, I think it was a girl, and she let me put my hand to her side and look deep into her eye."

He stopped for a moment to chew. "I don't know how to describe what it is I saw there. Maybe a whole future where I didn't have to farm anymore. Didn't have to plow or wish for rain or wish there wasn't rain. I didn't see an easy life or anything. I just saw a different one than what was planned out for me. So when the man tending the elephants came back and saw me, maybe that's why he didn't just throw me out on my ear."

"What did he do?"

"Offered me a job," Fred said with a smile. "Not a great one. Mucking out the elephant stalls for a pittance. But it would get me on the road out of town. Start my life off with the circus."

"So . . ." I racked my brain, trying to remember any stories I might have heard about a circus-traveling uncle. None came to mind. "Did you go?"

"I told him I'd think about it. Then I picked up and went back home to the farm."

"Back . . . What?" He wasn't meeting my eye. "What the heck did you do that for?"

"To think about it. Just like I told the man. I've been doing nothing but thinking about it ever since. Thinking's all I ever do, I guess." He picked himself up, and grasshoppers erupted in his wake. He held out a hand to help me up and saw the expression on my face. "Don't look so glum. A year or two later I did strike out on my own. Not with the circus, but around the country. Saw a lot of things, and it turned out okay. Now, come on. Let's get you on home."

I followed him but puzzled the whole time. It seemed there were things to my uncle that I'd never be able to understand. I'd never looked into the eye of an elephant. Didn't plan to either, but one time I'd looked into the eye of Gaucho when he was in a docile mood. I had pulled his head right over to me and looked him straight in the eye. Uncle Fred said there were no depths there, and I'm not saying he was wrong. But I saw something about myself in that eye. And it didn't have nothing to do with thinking for so long that I lost all my chances.

Twelve

I don't trust any place that smells fancier than me. Mimi says
it's the smell of paper and ink. Tree pulp and squid juice,
that's all it is. So that's what I kept repeating in my brain
as I stepped into the public library that hot day, where the
temperature turned from light broil to a mere chill just a few
steps past the doorframe. I almost never stepped foot in that
place, as I wasn't what you'd call a reader. I didn't care about
made-up stories, and when it came to real life, I learned most
of what I needed from looking and thinking. That had served
me fine in the past, but now things were different. I wasn't a
little kid anymore. Today I was on a mission.

"Tree pulp and squid juice . . . tree pulp and squid juice . . . tree pulp and squid juice . . ."

"Please tell me you're not mumbling about octopuses again," murmured Mimi.

I stuck my tongue out at her, which didn't give me courage as much as it decreased my nervousness. As I'd suspected, Mama was occasionally giving me a free afternoon when I'd been especially good at getting my chores done, and today was one of those days. I was fairly certain I was mere seconds from being tossed out as punishment for clearly not belonging in a place like this. It was all I could do to keep from tearing outta there, screaming my fool head off.

I tried desperately to figure out how I'd gotten myself into this pickle in the first place. I walked through it in my mind. At church the day before, I'd given Mimi her weekly update on our mysterious local ostrich owner, always making sure to add some new information.

"Madame Marantette was just like us. Then something changed and she went and became this star. I even saw a photograph of her kissing the king of England! Lip to lip," I said boldly, grateful I didn't have to meet Mimi's eyes. It could be tricky finding enough interesting facts about the Madame every week. "Probably," I said. Just to be safe.

"Did she really kiss the king?" asked Mimi incredulously.

Outside, after church, she was sitting behind me, engaged in one of her favorite activities: hair wrangling. Other folks might call it brushing or styling or what have you, but Mimi saw it for what it was. Wrangling. Of hair. Specifically mine. Most times I wouldn't concede to her torturous hands (I had a mother and an older sister to fill that role), but today I was just so full of vinegar that I had to talk to her one way or another.

"Don't know that they were lip to lip," I admitted, then waited the appropriate amount of time for Mimi to stop giggling behind me nervously. "What I do know is that she's a mystery."

"You tried asking her?" Mimi had a hairbrush out, and while I'd been talking, apparently peace talks with my hair had broken down and now it was all-out war. I wished I could have mediated between the two of them, but there's no negotiating with a woman bent on snarl annihilation.

"Asking her?" I scoffed, then indicated a memorial commemorating the Civil War dead, standing in the park across the street. "Go over there and ask Mr. Statue 'bout how he got out of this town and then got himself shot, why don't you? You'd get the same amount of information."

"So you haven't tried yet."

"Nothing *to* try," I muttered.

Mimi sighed. Then, "She's famous, right?"

"Certainly."

"Lots of stuff written up about her in the newspapers?"

"That's what happens when you're famous," I conceded.

"Then it's obvious. We go to the library. Read up on her. Figure it out."

So there we were. Next day even. There was no telling when I might ever be free again, and Mimi had a lot more experience than me with the library. Far as I knew, they didn't allow kids past the front door, but Mimi waved off my concerns. "That's from the old days," she said. "They let kids in all the time now. Only you gotta be clean. No coal dust on your fingers or anything, scuffing up the books. Besides"— she winked—"we're not children. We're researchers."

I was reasonably certain that excuse wasn't going to fly with the librarian standing behind the desk, eyeing us as we approached. The first thing I noticed about her was her glasses. I'd never seen anything like 'em. I'd seen glasses before, sure, but these weren't regular. The lenses were circles, but the metal holding them up crissed and crossed in an all-over kind of pattern. I found myself hypnotized, tracing their patterns up and over and down and up and—

"Well, good afternoon. I don't recall seeing you young ladies here before. How may I help you?" Her voice was crisp as the cold marble beneath our feet. My mind went completely blank. Mimi took a firmer hold on my arm, but she didn't say anything. This was my mission, after all.

"Begging your pardon, ma'am," I said, and darned if I didn't find myself going down into a curtsy again. Any more of this confronting-imperious-older-ladies business and I'd be curtsying to every cat and critter I came across in town.

The librarian inclined her head down slightly, waiting for me to continue.

"We'd like to do some research on . . ." I searched my brain for the exact phrasing Mimi and I had decided on hours earlier. ". . . on one of our local heroes."

"Ah!" The librarian's eyes lit up. Or maybe it was just how the sunlight hit her spectacles. "And which one have you selected?" School wasn't in session, but she was treating this like some kind of an assignment. I wasn't about to dissuade her of such a notion.

"Madame Marantette," I said.

Immediate silence. Now I couldn't see her eyes at all, thanks to the sunlit glare. Just glowing circles before a bunned head. She stood that way for a while and then uttered a quiet, "For research, then?"

"Research," I agreed.

"Not . . . gossip?"

"No!" I said it a little more forcefully than I should have, a bad move in a library. A couple of old men's heads poked up to glare from behind their newspapers, but the librarian looked like she believed me. Her mouth relaxed into a half smile, and then she walked around the desk.

"Easily done," she said. "We keep meticulous files on all the big names in the Three Rivers area. Marantette has been worth a case file of her own."

She led us into an adjacent room, filled with even more old men, all hunched and glaring.

The librarian unlocked a small room and disappeared inside. When she returned, she carried long boxes in her arms. They looked heavy, but she wielded them before her like she barely noticed their weight.

She placed them in the center of a table and opened the first to display the contents. Inside was a jumble of articles, photographs, posters, postcards, and whatnot. It took a little while for my eyes to adjust to the fact that the same woman appeared in each one. There sat the Madame, riding a horse. Not an average country rider, for there was no mistaking that steely spine. Her clothes were old-fashioned but undeniably fancy. Black puffed sleeves above an impossibly tiny corseted waist and, inexplicably, a man's silk top hat. Sometimes she was racing, sometimes she and the horse were jumping to ridiculous heights, but in all cases two things were true: She always wore a large silver brooch of a horse and rider at her throat, whether it was a photograph or an illustration. And in every single case, she rode sidesaddle.

"That's her all right," I said quietly. The librarian nodded.

"Here you'll find her past and her present. As for her future"—she patted another box on the table—"there's still plenty of room left."

She left us, and for the next few hours, Mimi and I plunged into the boxes. When we emerged, I had a picture in my mind.

Not a plan. But a picture's a pretty good start.

Thirteen

'll tell it the way I saw it, with headlines and articles and quotes from distinguished folk. It's messy, but I think the Madame's life was a little messy too, so that's all right.

NEWSPAPER #1

Local Girl Captures Eye of Talent Scout

Basically, this was how she got out of town in the first place. Emma (it feels wrong to call her that) had gotten pretty good at racing sidesaddle at the local county fairs. Then one day a scout for a small-time circus operation spotted her and signed her on the spot. It wasn't a big circus,

but it got her out of here and put her name out there.

NEWSPAPER #2

D. H. Harris Hires the

World's Greatest High Jump Champ:

Madame Marantette

Apparently, the Madame had gotten so good at races that she started showing off her jumping too. And that's when she got noticed by this D. H. Harris fellow, who'd make her jump higher and higher walls. Then they'd have a guy run out with a tape measure to show how high she'd jumped.

NEWSPAPER #3

Marantette Breaks High Jump

World Record

Madame Marantette jumped a seven-foot, ten-and-a-quarter-inch wall. Sidesaddle.

Fancy a Ride

in Your Own Train Car?

Travels with Madame Marantette

In this one, the reporter took a trip in the Madame's private railroad car, which was named St. Patrick after her favorite horse. Just like the photos I'd seen in the Madame's album.

NEWSPAPER #5

Marantette Performs Before Royalty,

Conquers the Whole of Europe

This article detailed the Madame's performance for the king of England. Apparently, it wasn't a private performance or anything. He just liked watching her so much that he'd visited the circus to see her a bunch of times. No photograph showing a kiss, though (believe me, Mimi checked).

And then the last one. Just a small piece from the local *St. Joseph County Times.*

NEWSPAPER #6

Madame Marantette Returns Home

This one I scanned for any sort of a clue as to why she came back, but I found nothing. Just said she was traveling home with her horses, ostriches, and dog.

She brought herself home to live in the middle of nowhere. Why?

Maybe it didn't matter. First things first, I told myself. One mystery at a time.

First, how to get out.

Then, later, worry about why you'd ever want to come back.

Fourteen

Bonnie Anne never signed up for any of this. If she could talk, she would probably want you to know that. Bud told me she'd had a pretty normal life for a mare prior to her purchase by the Madame. Born in the Bluegrass region of Kentucky, she was raised for running. Little did she suspect her future held a pulling partner roughly the height of a barn door, and a bird to boot. Every time she was hitched alongside Gaucho, I could almost see a little cloud of gloom form above the horse's head. Bonnie Anne could take directions. Gaucho wouldn't know a direction if it crawled into his head and danced the tarantella.

"The trick," Bud said to me one day after having given a deeply morose Bonnie Anne a brushing down, "might be in *what* you say to the bird." He walked with me out to the back pasture. "You know he can follow spoken directions, don't you?"

He could? We had just reached the fence and the ostriches were all eyeing us like we were lions closing in for the kill.

"Did you train him?" I asked hopefully. I still didn't know Bud all that well. All I knew about him came from Uncle Fred, and he was cagey with the info.

Bud shook his head at my question. "I'm a horseman, not an ostrich man. The Madame's the one that trained him, and she does a lot of talking to her animals. A bit like you."

"I try," I said. "It doesn't seem to do any good. Actually, there is something new I want to try today, though. Do you think I could get on Gaucho without the ladder or the fence?"

Bud cut me a skeptical glance. "How?"

"Well, I could grab the reins after you put 'em on him and just pull myself up. I have strong arms!" I showed him my muscles, but his raised eyebrow stayed fully cocked.

Uncle Fred, meanwhile, was bringing in the ostrich tack and ladder. Bud turned to him and called out, "She doesn't want to use the ladder today."

"The heck she doesn't" was all Uncle Fred replied.

I'd actually discussed this plan with Uncle Fred on the way down, and he'd dismissed it outright. "No reason you should make things harder on yourself."

"And what if I need to get on Gaucho and there's no ladder around? What then?"

"When would that ever happen?" Uncle Fred asked, flabbergasted.

I couldn't come up with a real reason, but I knew one existed somewhere out there. "It is best to be prepared," I declared loftily.

He snorted, neither agreeing nor disagreeing. I took that as a win. Uncle Fred did not.

Bud went to put the tack on Gaucho while Uncle Fred handed me the ladder. "Let it go, honey. No use doing the hard thing without any good reason."

"Maybe you just don't see the reason yet," I countered. "Maybe the reason's got its head hidden in the sand, and it'll pop up someday and surprise us."

"Ostriches don't actually bury their heads and reasons don't hide." He was dead serious. "Take the ladder, Suzy."

I took it. Took it and walked into that pasture up to the great big nine-foot-tall bird. "Good morning, Gaucho," I said cheerily. I'd gotten more used to talking to him in a casual manner since the early days. He turned his head to me, and his throat inflated, creating this strange *grrr*ing sound. Fred said when he did this, he was trying to sound like a lion. "Gaucho, you're not a lion," I informed him, not for the first time. "Or, if you are, you're a lion with a stuffy nose. Are you gonna be good for me today?"

I looked him over. By my estimation, those extra four feet he had on me were all for show. He didn't need 'em, and I didn't need to mind 'em.

I lowered my voice a little. "Today we're gonna try something new. You ready for this?"

He had, at this point, realized a little belatedly that I was not just any Loud Small Person but *his* Loud Small Person, and he stopped hooting at me.

Making a big show of it, I flung the ladder to one side, grabbed the reins, and launched myself, leg up, toward his back, yelling all the while, "Up, up, Gaucho!"

I didn't even get halfway there before the whole kit and caboodle (which is to say, me, myself, and I) came crashing right back down to the ground. I stood up, not sure if I was more furious with myself or with the ding-dang bird. A chorus of hoots erupted from the two men behind me. Something about the sheer confidence of my attitude and my complete and utter failure (to say nothing of the fact I was clearly unharmed) struck 'em as pretty much the funniest thing they'd seen in an age. Bud was hanging off the fence guffawing, while Uncle Fred was hanging on to it for dear life, trying to gasp out some sort of encouraging words to me and failing utterly.

My pride had been bruised, not broken. I decided to try again. And again. And again, each time assuring Uncle Fred and Bud that I was unharmed, until I was lying there on the ground within stomping distance of Gaucho, who, despite everything, did not appear to be in a stomping kind of mood. I optimistically chalked that up to him growing fond of me in some way. The truth of the matter is that maybe he just didn't deem me stomp-worthy. But the worst of it was that the darned ostrich wasn't even the problem. He was so used to me getting on his back by this point that he just stood there, letting me take the failure all on my lonesome.

I started spitting and cursing. "Ooooooh, you ornery, no-good, lousy, dumb-eyed, flea-bitten, smelly, old . . ."

Suddenly the hilarity in front of me stopped cold.

I turned to see the Madame herself.

She looked at me down on the ground in the dirt, from where I'd been swearing at Gaucho like a drunken sailor, and proceeded to enter the pasture.

"Gaucho. Come." She slapped her hand to her side in one swift, sure movement. With only a moment's hesitation he trotted forward, coming to rest before her. She picked up the reins.

"Now, watch out, Madame. He may—"

"I would not presume to tell me how to handle my bird if I were you, Mr. Bowles."

"No, Madame!" Uncle Fred sputtered a little, removed his hat, and backed off a couple steps, so that I felt sorry for the fellow. My frustration with the bird began to turn to a frustration with the Madame, but before I could say anything, she was approaching me with Gaucho in tow.

"Stand up, Suzy," she said.

I stood.

"In my time I have owned many steeds. But none can compare to my Gaucho. He was acquired young, but full-grown, and it is a miracle that he came into my possession at all considering the viciousness of his character. He was just one of the flock my husband, Daniel, bestowed upon me as a gift, but right from the start it was clear that Gaucho was different. There is a fire in him that sets him apart, and it did not take me long to realize that this was a fire I could fan.

"He is not," she continued, "the most intelligent animal. You should note that, for reasons God alone knows, his eyeballs are larger than his brain. However, even an overgrown hen is capable of learning commands. Moreover, there is a joy I feel from him when he runs." She turned to me suddenly. "Have you observed that?"

I had noticed the joy Gaucho took in throwing me off

when he ran, but I knew that wasn't what she meant, so I said nothing. When I didn't respond, she just sighed.

"A joy. I tapped into it early on, and I suspect that until you or the men here understand how to release that joy, we will all have a time of it getting him to pair with my sweet Bonnie Anne." She broke off from what she was saying to smile suddenly. "I saw it first when he raced the middle-distance champion of the world, Percy Smallwood, in a foot-race in the Pittsburgh, Pennsylvania, Hippodrome. I don't need to tell you who won. Come." She beckoned to me with her free hand. "Allow me to give you some advice on how to train an animal."

Gaucho shifted his steps with me so close but didn't attack or flee, and the Madame approached his other side, stroking the feathers on his back.

"When I was training my horses to jump, I observed early on how the other trainers did it. Their methods were cruel and swift. Whips were not unusual by any means. One of my greatest horses, Filemaker, came to me thin and wary. But with patience and kindness I won him over. Now, do you know, Suzy, why people fall off horses when they attempt high jumps?"

This was a trick question, but I didn't feel like traipsing around the edge of it and figured it would save us both time if I just fell straight in. "Because they don't hold on hard enough?"

"Not at all. You might as well hold as tightly as you like but that will not prevent your body from careening through space." She waved my answer away like a bad smell. "Why do they fall? THAT is the key to riding. Nine times out of ten they do not trust the horse. They do not listen to the horse. They do not understand that the horse has the correct instincts in place to attempt the jump on their own. This bird," she said resolutely, "is no horse. But he has instincts. Instincts that you must trust. Or . . ." She looked thoughtful. ". . . completely suffocate." Pause. "One or the other could work." She handed me his reins. "See that you ride him sidesaddle."

Then she turned on her heel and walked out of the pasture.

I looked at Bud, who—darn him—was doing that kind of laugh where you don't make any sound out loud but your shoulders keep heaving up and down real fast.

"He can really take commands?" I asked, indicating the bird.

Bud stopped his silent laughter and nodded. "Sure. I told you that. Commands for the surrey. Don't think anyone's ever bothered teaching him commands for riding him."

I considered this. "Can I have a feed bag?"

Uncle Fred ran back to fetch it from the stables. Meanwhile I lowered Gaucho's head so's I could look right smack dab in his eye.

"All right. Bird. Here's how it's gonna go. I'm gonna talk to you even more now. You think you're already sick of it? Just get ready. Every single minute I'm on that back of yours it'll just be talky talky talk talk talk. I don't think there's a book on how to train an ostrich." I paused. Maybe there was one at the library? I filed that away for later. "But whatever the case, I'm training you, bird." Then, in a quieter voice, "I think you're my ticket out of here."

Not that I would be riding him sidesaddle or anything. I wasn't that desperate. Not yet.

Uncle Fred walked over to me with the bag. Gaucho didn't know much, but he knew one thing: bag equals bad. I imagined him saying to himself, "No bag. No bag. No bag," as he shimmied backwards, his big old dinosaur feet picking up and dropping in double-quick time. He even hissed a couple times in warning, which, from an ostrich, sounds like someone sucking the last drops of a drink with a straw.

"Gimme," I said to Uncle Fred, but he didn't hand it to me.

"There's a trick to it, Suzy. You'd best let me—"

"Gimme," I repeated. I snatched the bag out of his hands as Gaucho pulled away from me.

"Okay, lesson one!" I shouted as he pulled me faster and faster by the reins to the back end of the pasture. "The bag is good. Repeat! The bag is good! We like the bag! The bag is our friend!"

He wasn't buying it, so I modulated my tone to make it honey-sweet instead of panicky.

"Good bag. Nice bag. Pretty bag." Of course, by now he had been distracted by one of the other ostriches standing perilously close to where he'd wanted to pull me mere minutes ago. Bag forgotten, he was now puffing up his feathers in a warlike display. As I inched closer to his head, I decided that now would be a good time to try that new trick from the morning. Maybe my problem was that I was trying to get onto his back from a cold stop next to him. Maybe the real trick meant running, jumping, and pulling all at the same time. With a firm grip on the reins, I backed up, then took a flying leap onto his back with my customary "Up, up, Gaucho!"

From the moment I landed, I realized two things at the same time: First, that landing on Gaucho's back now got a different reaction out of him than it used to. True, I could feel him tense up below me, ready to run, but, I dunno how to describe it. The tension wasn't . . . tense? The next thing I realized was that I had precisely one second to get that bag on. Once he took off there wouldn't be a way to bounce and jounce and aim precisely enough to swoop it over his pecky little beak.

The instant my leg swung over his back, I got my arm around and bagged his head up. Immediately his puffed-up feathers relaxed. Even the ostrich he'd been facing calmed down, clearly under the impression that the big, scary opponent it had been facing had miraculously disappeared. No head, no threat.

I cooed into the bag, "That's right. That's right, Gaucho.

It's nice in the bag. It's not scary. Now we're gonna practice commands, yep."

I paused. I had no idea what commands he already knew or what commands you were supposed to do with an ostrich. I figured I'd keep it simple and get straight to the point.

"Gaucho. Walk," I said, and dug my heels into his side a little.

Gaucho did not walk.

"Gaucho. Walk!" I said with a little more force.

Gaucho turned his head as if to say, "Is someone calling my name?" then decided he was just hearing things and went back to staring into the inside of the bag.

"Oh, for crying out loud!"

This went on for a while. Occasionally he'd walk a little, and I'd get excited and think he was understanding, but then it would be clear that he was just stretching his legs for the fun of it.

"Suzy," I heard Uncle Fred call from the fence. "We don't have a ton of time before we have to get back to the farm. Best to let him tire out."

"Fine!" I snapped. "Gaucho?" I whipped off his bag. "Run, Gaucho! Run!"

He took off like a shot, me yelling, "Run! Run! Run!" the whole way.

Sometimes that bird took pretty good directions.

Fifteen

On the whole, my family didn't bring up my trips to the Marantette house, excepting my granny, of course. She kept mentioning it at the dinner table so that she could pull out phrases like "no better than she oughta" about the Madame. I didn't quite understand what those phrases meant but figured they weren't all that nice. Still, considering my family's practice in ignoring Granny, if anything they probably felt happy that I'd given her something new to complain about.

Since I had Mama and Daddy's permission, Granny's anger didn't scare me. Not with her talk anyway.

My brother Bill still scared me, though. He scared me 'cause I was smart enough to know to be scared.

I figured that when he learned I was going out with Uncle Fred every morning, he'd do anything he could to squash it. But that's the thing with evil geniuses. They do what you fear, but not what you expect.

He started small by insulting Uncle Fred. "He's actually a lot worse than dumb," Bill said outside the privy, where I couldn't escape him. "Did he tell you that he was a cowboy? You know that's a lie, right? I heard he was a clown in a rodeo for a while, and even that job he mucked up. You can't believe a word he says."

When these lies didn't get me going, he figured maybe it was the Madame who was the lure. He started calling her all the names Granny came up with and worse ones that I didn't even know the definitions of. It didn't make me raise so much as an eyebrow. But Bill's got a genius for knowing where your softest skin will feel the sharpest pinch.

It was a Wednesday. I was just sitting down to lunch. With the possible exception of breakfast, any meal in my home is a bit on the loud side. That's 'cause with six kids and five adults all living under the same roof, squeezing everyone in and then getting what you want on the table requires an awful lot of haggling. On this particular day, Bill sat down to my right.

After grace was said and the family volume increased, he started in.

"I finally figured it out. Why you go over there. Took me a while. Then it all just clicked." He had a mixed expression on his face. Two parts pity, one part concern. He put his hand on my wrist, gently. "You think you can be like her, don't you?"

"What?" I whipped my hand away.

Bill, serving himself some salted potatoes to go with his soup, pressed on. "I get it. You've got these ideas about yourself that you don't belong here. Why else would you have this under your bed?" And with the flourish of some dark arts magician, he pulled out of his sleeve an old yellowed piece of newsprint. It was the tiny map from under my bed. The red-haired rat had scared up my secret collection.

"Give me that!" I hissed, but it disappeared back up his shirt sleeve, and Bill's fake big-brother face was replaced with a look of greedy triumph that appeared only when one of his jabs finally hit home.

"That's it, isn't it?" he said. "You think you can get out of this town someday. Like this Madame Marantette lady's gonna do something to help you. Here's the thing." And he leaned in real close, like he was divulging the secrets of the spheres.

What he said next gave voice to every fear in my head. After that day, whenever I doubted myself, that doubting voice in my head was Bill's voice.

"You're never getting away. You're staying here just like everybody else. Nobody leaves here for good. Nobody."

He was driving a nail into the part of me that squished, and I couldn't help but try to counter him.

I turned to him, teeth gritted. "Well, the Madame did. She got out. She was just old plain Emma Peek and then she left and traveled the world and saw things and did things. So someone can get out if they want."

"Wrong," he said, spearing a thick slab of ham and poking it into his mouth.

"Smaller bites, Bill," said our mother's warning voice from down the table. "And, Suzy, dear? Eat your lunch."

"Sure she left," he said, softer now. "Maybe she even did some of the stuff she says, though I bet she's lying half the time." He stopped chewing and looked me dead in the eye.

"But she came back. She. Came. Back. Even though she's got no friends and no family in this town and half the people here hate her anyway. She still had to come back. 'Cause even if you're the most famous person in the world, you don't get to belong anywhere but where you started from." He took a chomp of a roll. "Not really."

I tried to come up with a counter-argument and failed. It didn't occur to me until years later that he was so convincing because this was also the story he'd been forcing himself to hear.

I managed to choke down the remainder of the meal, though I don't think I tasted a thing. When I tried to excuse myself, I heard my mother's voice call out, "Suzy, it's your turn to do the dishes after lunch."

Without a word, I snatched up the plates and stomped into the kitchen. Even in my foul mood, I had enough sense not to break them (though I really, really wanted to try). *Bill. Thinking he's so smart. Thinking he knows everything. He doesn't know anything.* He wasn't even that much older than me, and he definitely wasn't smarter.

So how come I knew he was right?

I'd filled the sink with the plates and had started scraping the leftovers into the slop barrel when I sensed someone lingering in the doorway. I spun on my heel, ready to fling a dirty plate at Bill's smirk-soaked head, only to find my sweet mama standing there instead.

"Just come by to see how you're doing."

"I'm doing fine," I huffed. I kept on with my scraping. I heard her leave through the back door. Then, a couple minutes later, she came back in with water from the pump.

"Like a hand?" she asked. "These chores can sometimes take over your day, I know."

She wasn't wrong about that. I knew I hadn't really thought through what I'd signed on for. Some days I found myself working from before sunrise to dinnertime, collapsing on my bed right after, and sleeping so deep that I could have given Dotty some tips. Uncle Fred had taken to waking me in the morning so I didn't have to do it myself, but that didn't make my body any happier when it realized I was abandoning a nice soft bed for a hard dirt road.

I felt a wave of gratitude toward my mama, and side by side we started in on the washing. Bill's words were still gnawing, but they'd lost a little of their bite.

I glanced over at Mama. No one ever left here. Maybe. But people left other places.

"Mama?"

"Hm?"

"Were you really a photographer's assistant back in Oklahoma?"

A slow, thoughtful nod. "Pretty much."

"Wow." I knew that but hadn't thought much about it. "You take photos of anyone famous?"

She laughed. "Child, I was a studio photographer's assistant. We took photos of people on their wedding day or family shots. Or babies. We did a lot of babies."

"Babies?" I frowned. "How'd you do that? Wasn't it hard to get them to sit still and look all sweet?"

"It was. But you see, Mr. Sones, that was the photographer

I worked for, he had a surefire method of getting babies happy for their photos. Made him the most popular man in the state for baby photography."

"What was his secret?" I asked eagerly. "Did he drug them?"

"Did he drug . . . No, Suzy! No! I mean, he might have wanted to," she tittered, then stopped herself when she realized how unseemly it was. "No, I was his secret weapon. Me!"

"How so?" I looked her over. "You didn't even have babies then."

"No, but I did have a lot of little brothers and sisters. That meant I knew how to hold a baby. So you see, what we'd do is, we had this chair that we draped a big piece of fabric over. I'd sit in the chair and he'd put the fabric over me. Then he'd put the baby on my lap, and I'd kind of hold it up and nuzzle it and sing to it a little and try to make it sit still long enough for the exposure to set in."

The thought of my mother sitting like some kind of furniture ghost holding other people's babies caused me to explode into giggles right there at the sink.

She let me go on like this a good minute or two before she finally said, "All right. All right. You got it out of you. Your mama had a goofy job. I admit it."

"Is that . . ." I sniffed and wiped my nose on the back of my hand. "Is that all you did, then? Just pretend to be a really comfy chair?" She swatted me playfully with her wet hand, which I fended off.

"Certainly not. I was trained to process all the exposures and probably inhaled more darkroom chemicals than was strictly healthy. Sometimes the photographer let me do everything, from the shoot to the processing, by myself. I could have run my own shop by the end, you know."

"Really?" A woman-owned photography studio would be something else. "Why didn't you?"

"Met your father, didn't I? He came rolling in there like he didn't have a care in the world, took one look at me, and the rest is history."

"Did you put a sheet over yourself and have him sit on your lap . . . ?"

"Okay, that's it, young lady, now you're getting it." The next ten minutes consisted of Mama merrily trying to get the lye soap into my mouth and me fending her off with the bristle brush we saved for such occasions. By the time Granny walked in to see what all the fuss was about, we were both covered in suds and so thoroughly silly that she took one look, turned on her heel, and walked out again, which just set us off for good.

It wasn't until later that night when I was curled up in my bed that I thought back to all that Mama had done. She'd learned some real skills once. She'd been a photographer. Knew the ins and outs of it.

But what good was it now except as stories to tell your kids?

I loved my home. I really did. But what if what Bill said was true? Maybe he was right. Maybe leaving at all would be foolish, because what was the point if you just had to come back to where you started?

Staring up into the darkness, I made a vow. I mean, there was only one thing left for it.

I had to talk to the Madame.

Sixteen

I missed Mimi.

The whole extra-farm-chores deal lost a lot of its sparkle early on. Occasionally I'd be bent over, washing the floor in the kitchen or something, and then Bill would saunter in, all casual. He'd just stand there and stare at me and say absolutely nothing until the heat of his gaze burned the back of my neck so bad that I'd just look at him and scream, "What? WHAT?" He'd just smile real slow. Then back out of the room, his eyes never leaving mine.

"Worth it?" he'd call over his shoulder.

And it was. But barely. I missed roaming the farm on my

own. I missed sitting in trees doing nothing. I missed my best friend.

It was the day after my talk with Mama when I had a particularly trying time with Gaucho. I was beginning to despair of ever figuring out what went on in that miraculously small noggin of his. And I knew I had to have a talk with the Madame about all sorts of things. The unspoken rule at our weekly teas was that we would not talk "business" while there, and "business" in this case meant "Gaucho." Even so, I was fixing on getting her opinion on that darned bird one way or another at the next meeting.

After Uncle Fred and I got back to our farm, I stumbled to the dining room just in time for lunch.

"WARSH!" Granny growled at me. Sometimes she says the word with an "r" and sometimes she doesn't, and I've never quite been able to figure out what makes it pop out. Mama says she does it because some of her family came from Ohio long ago. All's I know is, there ain't no "r" in "wash."

After saying grace, Daddy called over, "Suzy, come see me after lunch about your afternoon chores."

"Yes, sir," I said, groaning. Daddy's chores were usually harder on a body than Mama's. Sometimes he figured I was just a child-sized beast of burden, and sometimes he saw a living, breathing kid. I was never quite sure which it would be. Maybe, I fantasized as I ate, I'd get something soft and gentle like helping with a batch of cookies or tidying up the pantry. Turned out, it was much better than all of that.

"Why don't you take off for today and go visit Mimi."

I could hardly believe my ears. Just stood and blinked like I was staring into a white-hot sun.

"Go on, now. Get! Before your granny figures out what I've done."

I tore out the back screen door, letting it bang behind me in the way that Granny didn't like, and pelted toward Mimi's. It was like when a rabbit sees a hound dog coming and runs its fool legs off. I was that bunny, with the threat of Granny a hound dog at my heels.

Mimi's farm isn't all that far off from my own. Just about a mile south, if you know where to hop the occasional creek.

Mimi's little sister, Gertrude, was the first to spot me.

"MIMI! MIMI! SUZY'S HERE! SUZY'S HERE FOR YOU, MIMI!"

It was like looking at a kitten and discovering it was a foghorn in disguise. Nothing readies you for those lungs.

Mimi's mama poked her head out the door and grinned wide. "SUZY! IT'S BEEN AN AGE! CAN I GET YOU A CINNAMON ROLL OR A DOUGHNUT?" This was followed swiftly by a chorus of voices in the house saying, "HEY! I WANT A DOUGHNUT!"

"Thank you, ma'am. I just ate," I said.

Mimi flew out the door, matching her mama with a quick "WE'RE OFF TO THE FIELDS, MAMA, I'LL SEE YOU LATER!"

"DON'T FORGET TO FOLD THE HANGING LINENS ON YOUR WAY BACK!" said Mrs. Aynuk as we darted away.

"Phew!" said Mimi, all normal-voiced when we could only hear the faintest of reverberations from her home. "Been trying to find an excuse to get out of there all morning. How'd you know to rescue me?"

I grinned. "Just good timing. Daddy set me free today from chores."

Mimi was no fool. "Those would be the chores you agreed to? The chores that keep you from ever seeing your best friend except at church and the occasional library run?"

"Those are the ones," I said, feeling a twinge of guilt.

She didn't respond. Mimi and I used to meet up all the

time together. Now here I was signing away my time without thinking about how it would affect her at all.

"Sorry," I said belatedly as we walked.

She gave me a wink, which helped my heart rise a tidbit. Then she stopped cold. "I know we planned this together, but I thought you'd just talk to the Madame and that would be it. Instead you're over at her place all the time. Every single day. I can't quite figure out what you're up to, Ms. Helen Susan Bowles."

Uh-oh. She was using my full name. The one she swore never to use in front of other people and to only invoke in the direst of circumstances. This was serious.

"Why would a healthy girl of twelve want to spend all her time over at a circus performer's house, even if she was world-famous? There's something going on with you, Suzy B., and I want in on it." She plunked herself down on the nearest stump. "Spill."

I'd never told anyone about my dream to get off the farm, out of Burr Oak, into the wider world. I'd hardly even told myself, not even when Bill pulled my secret map from his ratty old sleeve, but I decided to tell my best friend everything. While I spoke, Mimi would occasionally make this little "hm" sound. Like some of it she'd guessed herself and just needed confirmation on.

"What you're telling me is that you want to see the world.

The Madame *has* seen the world. So you plan on riding this ostrich, and somehow by doing that, and having tea with a woman who keeps telling you to sit up straight, you're going to somehow use all of this to . . ." She trailed off.

"I haven't worked out all the details yet," I confessed.

Mimi sat there a moment or two, thinking to herself. We watched a woolly bear caterpillar inch its stubborn way across the path before us.

"*I* don't want to get out," she finally said.

"No one said you had to."

"But we were born in the same place. Both of us have lots of relatives around. You never said anything about hating it before. Your family is here and your friends are here."

"Yep. And I don't hate it!" I was quick to point this out.

She went on like she hadn't heard me. "We go to the same church and eat the same food and go to the same fairs and know the same folks."

I didn't say anything.

"So why is it that you want to go but I'm happy here?" She looked at me with pure consternation on her face. Like it was hurting her to not know the answer to this simplest of questions. "Why do you want to go at all?"

"You see that ratty old scarecrow over there?" I said, pointing to a scarecrow in the cornfield.

She snorted. "Pa's constantly putting scarecrows up, but

he always forgets to replace 'em. I think that one's something like number fifty-two."

"Doesn't it remind you a bit of that scarecrow in that book you used to read to me? *The Wonderful Wizard of Oz*?"

"You wouldn't want to go to Oz with that scarecrow." She nodded her head at the field. "He'd collapse on you before you could set a foot on the yellow brick road."

"Yeah, but you know how that book begins? With Kansas being all dried up and brown and the sun just fades all the colors there?"

"We don't live in Kansas," Mimi said, logically enough. "Michigan has more color than we know what to do with."

"But see, here's the thing." I leapt up and started pacing, excited by what I was coming to realize. "Dorothy wouldn't know a lucky tornado if it picked her up and dropped her seven stories down. You know how she got to Oz? She crawled into bed and then she got taken somewhere else without even having to leave her pillow. Me? I can't stay in one spot. This is all beautiful." And I swung my arm wildly at the trees and corn and sky. "But it's not going anywhere. I am."

She could have dug in. She could have kept up her side of the argument about why it was better here than anywhere else in the world, and I would have listened. I almost wanted to be convinced. It was a lot easier to accept your fate if someone else told you you were supposed to take the easier road.

I could see Mimi weighing what it meant to *keep* her good friend versus what it meant to *be* a good friend. And with Mimi, the being always won out.

"Then you need a plan."

The next Monday I had tea with the Madame.

Seventeen

"Madame? I have to know something."

So maybe it wasn't the most complicated plan in the world. Mimi had seen right away that what I needed and really wanted to know was how a girl born in this part of the world could get away. "Just ask her," she said. "Maybe there's a secret to it. She's gotta talk to you about something other than whether your pinky is extended high enough when you drink tea." What Mimi didn't really realize what that my teas with the Madame were already about more than simple manners. I noticed how the Madame would always pepper our lessons with other kinds of advice. She might explain to me that etiquette demanded that thank-you letters never contain the words "thank you," then say on the sly something confusing about how I "should never confuse gratitude with debt" in either myself or others. I suspected that just like I was trying to teach Gaucho how to be a good bird without him dumping me, she was trying to teach me how to be a better person without me dumping her advice. She'd even drop in some knowledge about handling Gaucho from time to time, like the fact that if I ever found a tomato hornworm caterpillar, I should save it for him because those were his favorite treats.

But to my simple statement, the Madame said nothing.

I soldiered on. "You went all over the world when you were with the circus, didn't you?"

"All over the world?" she repeated softly, then shook her head. "Only most of America and parts of Europe, my dear. That was, of course, before I retired. Posture, Suzy. You are slumping again."

"Retired?"

"Retired," she confirmed. "Quit forever. I am not, as you may have noticed, in the circus any longer."

I had noticed. However, I suddenly realized what this meant.

"So . . ." I looked down at the ground, fumbling for words. They'd abandoned me in my time of need. "You don't work for Ringling Brothers anymore? You couldn't . . ." I stopped myself then. What was I trying to ask? That she recommend me to them? Get me a job in the circus? Was that why I'd been riding her ostrich all this time? It was, I realized with a shock.

The Madame smiled. "Do you know why I wanted a field of ostriches behind my home?"

The question caught me off guard. Fact was, I hadn't really thought to wonder that.

"Well . . . you were with the circus before."

"Do you think that everyone who works for the circus takes a dozen ostriches home as a parting gift?"

She was having fun with me, and something about knowing that the Madame had a sense of humor made me relax a hair.

"Posture."

I un-relaxed. "So why did you want them?"

She took a deliberate sip from her cup. "I do not talk

about my husband Daniel very often, but he was the love of my life while he was alive. A late-in-life love." She indicated a framed photograph on the table across from us. "You can see him there."

It was the mustachioed man I'd seen before. He looked like

a banker. I stared at it an extra-long time so that she would think I was getting something out of the experience.

Yep. Banker.

"Daniel was my manager for a long time, and one day he turned to me and said, 'Emma. I want to give you something to remember me by.'" Then he placed a blindfold over my eyes and led me out to the back paddock. When he released the blindfold, I saw before me twelve ostriches, the most stunning samples I'd ever seen before."

"Did you have ostriches in the circus?" I asked.

"No. And I had never had an opinion on them, honestly. My riding had been done with horses. It wasn't until Daniel's gift that I began to take a greater interest in ostriches. Do you know," she said, warming to the subject, "that when facing down a lion, they fan out their wings to look larger?" I thought of Gaucho making little lion noises at me whenever he got ruffled. I wondered how much of his small brain was spent thinking about lions. She sat back. "There is much to learn about our friend the ostrich. Indeed, if you wish to understand Gaucho completely so that you may ride him to success, you would do well to learn as much about him as possible."

"But . . . can't you just teach me about him?" I sputtered. "Seems like you're the one who knows the most about him."

"Knowledge is best acquired firsthand. If you are going to ride Gaucho truly, then you must study him, inside and out."

How the heck was I gonna go and do that if she wasn't about to tell me?

The whole time she'd been going on about the ostriches, the question I had wanted to ask had reappeared and been flaring up in my head, so much that now I couldn't make it go back down.

"Madame, why did you come back here?"

For a moment she didn't answer me. Didn't even look at me. Just gazed straight ahead. Like she could see through the walls at the swaying fields, so full of bees that the chorus sounded less like wings and more like a conversation held at a pitch out of range of our ears. At the blue-skied day and the trill of cicadas and birdsong.

"I never had to come back. But if you don't go back to where you are from, how else can you remember where you've been?" She turned her eyes to meet mine. "It is not a punishment to live here, even if I never planned it when I was young. Someday, Suzy, you may be called upon to make a great sacrifice to achieve what you truly want."

And we finished our tea. And I left the house. And she shut the door. And I didn't think then that I was any nearer to answers than I had been before.

Eighteen

Sometimes folks act like they've got me all figured out. They were young once, so they think there's some wisdom they've tapped into, just because the world has spun beneath their feet a couple more times than mine. They look at me and think I'm just some overalls-wearing farm girl who's gonna get hit by the puberty stick someday and instantly turn into this gracious little lady with frills and bows and sweet-smelling talcums galore.

Sometimes I think they might be right.

I was thinking maybe they could be right the day my sister Mary suggested we do ourselves up right and proper and go into town as fancy as possible. As I might have mentioned before, Mary doesn't have much in the way of friends around these parts, and she's always itching to age me up about four years or so, so we can be best bosom buddies. Normally, I don't go for it, but I'd been getting the Madame's "comportment" lessons for a while now, and it occurred to me that this might be the perfect excuse to put them to the test. So, for once in my life, I let Mary have her way.

After Mary conned Ernest into giving us a ride to town, I made sure to keep my back straight like the Madame had instructed me. I felt poised. I did not belch or scratch or spit or pick at my nails. Mary noted this change, and I could see she approved of it.

"You're getting more like a grown lady every day," she said as we jounced a little in the cart. "I wonder that I didn't notice it before."

I swallowed an urge to fiddle with my dress and smiled back at her. "There's a lot about me you don't know," I said.

Mary laughed out loud. "Oh, really?" She was amused by the notion. "Well, tell me what you've been up to, then."

"I've been learning how to be a lady from Madame Marantette," I said, hoping to get a bit of a reaction out of her.

And she did raise her eyebrows in surprise, but then she looked more curious than anything else. "The circus woman you've been working for with Uncle Fred? Daddy said you'd been doing chores for her or something. What's learning to be a lady have to do with any of that?"

"Well, it's kind of a trade-off," I started. Then stopped. It occurred to me that maybe I didn't want to go flaunting my hijinks with Gaucho all over the place. Not when I'd just gotten Mary's approval all of a sudden. I could not see my refined older sister approving of her younger sibling bumping all over the countryside on the back of an ostrich. I felt a little sad about it, but my secrets were not for my sister.

"I do odd jobs for her and she teaches me about . . . comportment," I said quickly.

"Comportment?" Mary looked even more amused. "Well, I don't know much about this Madame Marantette woman, but if that's what she's doing for you, then I'm glad you've gotten to know her."

The grin on my face sustained me all the rest of the way into town. That is, until we encountered the women.

It took me a long time to figure out that gossip, otherwise known as the spitting of words that may or may not be true but seem to carry with them information that no one else in the world may have, is currency to a bored brain. If you have discovered something gossip-worthy, it is your sworn duty as a member of these here United States of America to pass it along to your friends and enemies, to show them how much more you know about the state of the world today than they. I don't truck with gossip. Unless it's interesting, of course. Then I'm all ears.

Still, I don't think I quite realized that I would be a most valuable source of the stuff until the moment I found myself walking down the street with Mary and we were set upon by a mighty crew of biddies. A biddy, for the record, is a woman who sees gossip more like air than food. You can live a while without food. You get my meaning.

By the time I realized we were surrounded, it was far too late. These biddies were our mother's age, mostly, every one of them a member of our church, and each with a corvid gleam in her eye.

"Mary and Suzy! Look at these fine young ladies that are joining us today!" cooed Mrs. Raphus, the minister's wife and a chronic hugger. I was enveloped almost instantly and lost sight of the world I knew for a good thirty seconds.

Upon my release, Mrs. Goura caught my cheek in a tight pinch, murmuring, "We've been hearing lots of fine stories about your adventures lately, Suzy."

"Adventures?" I gasped, for Mrs. Phaps had gathered my hands together in a tight squeeze that was, I could already tell, going to last an additional thirty seconds that I'd never get back.

"Don't be shy with us," Mrs. Phaps tittered. "We all know

how you and tha—how you and your uncle have been going down to the old Marantette place every morning at dawn. My, oh my, what DO you get up to over there?"

"And what does that woman get up to?" This was uttered by the far-more-timid Mrs. Ganter, newly married as of this past March. She was just eighteen but already working hard on her matronly features, and far too direct in her curiosity.

"Merriam!" Mrs. Raphus scolded. Then she softened. "We don't hold with gossip of that sort. Just checking in on one of our favorite girls and what she's been up to, that's all."

"Oh, she's in the Marantette house every day!"

I turned in slow shock. My own sister. Mary. Spilling the beans as fast as she could. I realized in that moment that, on our ride up, I had inadvertently given her a sow's ear full of quantifiable gossip to peddle. Unlike every other woman here, I had actually been in the Madame's house. Had spoken with her face to face. Had sipped her tea. So as I stood frozen, I watched my sister transform before my eyes, from maiden to matron. It was like I could see into her future. She would wed, sure she would. Wed and have as many children as her house could hold. Her dresses would grow large and comfortable and formless as her mind grew large and comfortable and formless. And this gossip she now gave away so freely was bound to be something she drank in desperation later on.

I shook my head a little, and the vision passed. Shook my head so that I wouldn't look down at my own self, dressed so similarly to Mary. So I wouldn't see myself transform in that way as well. *You can't transform,* I thought, *if you don't stay.*

I had to get away. Not out of the town right now, but away from these women.

I'm not one to rule out the possibility of miracles. They seem as likely a thing to happen as anything else I've seen in this world. I was now in desperate straits, knowing full well that the biddies were mere moments away from turning their eyes upon me, demanding in soft, sweet, irresistible ways for me to confess everything I knew about the Madame. Trouble was, where could I go? Who would take in a twelve-year-old escapee? Then, like the parting of the Red Sea before Moses, Mrs. Goura and Mrs. Ganter both, simultaneously, unconsciously, took a step back, and in that gap I saw it. My sanctuary.

The library.

"MaryIhavetodosomeresearchforMimiatthelibraryI'llonlybeaminuteseeyoutherebye!"

I dived for the gap, which had now begun to slowly close, the women mere seconds from cutting off my escape route. Sacrificing a sprig of baby's breath that Mary had lovingly placed in my locks not one hour before, I abandoned all my ladylike demeanor and tore down the street to the library like the devil himself was nipping at my heels.

By the time I burst through the doors into the incredible cool, I was undoubtedly red-faced, panting, and unaccountably, undeniably free.

Nineteen

The old men in the room turned and faced me as one. Then they all turned back. Nothing more to see here.

The librarian was in her usual place at the desk and smiled at me as I approached. "Suzy, isn't it?"

I was incapable of speech, so I just indicated that it was indeed me.

"Where's your friend today?"

I ignored the question, realizing all at once that I truly did have a reason to be there.

"I want everything you have on ostriches!" I gasped.

"Ostriches?" The librarian went into think mode. I later figured out that this is a fun thing they do. Try it on one sometime. You ask them a question and then they get all still and try to figure out where to find the stuff you need. She stood there, stock-still, for about twenty seconds, then turned on her heel and walked away. I wasn't certain if I should follow or not, but the *click, click, click* of her shoes was so decisive that I figured it would be foolish not to.

She took me straight into the stacks, where the books smelled particularly nice, and ran her finger delicately over the spines. After a moment, she plucked out a book titled *Ostriches and Ostrich Farming.* "There we are," she said triumphantly. "One book on ostriches for you."

☆ ☆ ☆

I blew across the top of the book, and a cloud of dust wafted away from me. "How old is this?"

She plucked the book from my hands and checked. "1877. Too old?"

Granny had been a young woman when this had been released. "I guess ostriches haven't changed that much."

"That's the spirit," she said. "Let me know if there's anything else you need."

"Can I have a pencil and paper?" No harm in asking, and as it happened she gave me exactly that.

By the time Mary located me, I was scribbling away on

my paper at a table with one old man on one side of me and another old man on the other. She approached the table with venom in her eyes, but when all three of us looked up at her slowly, she seemed to lose a goodly portion of her nerve.

"Suzy! What are you doing?" she hissed.

"Working," I murmured. "Can I stay another hour?"

I felt a little sorry for her. We had started the day with her hoping for some fun sister time. Now here I was, shoulder to shoulder with a bunch of longbeards, taking notes on a dusty tome while outside the fresh air and sunshine beckoned.

"Is that really what you want?" she whispered, incredulous.

The old man to my left raised a finger and began to shush her, but I put a hand on his arm and said, "It's all right, Cornelius. That's my sister Mary. She's not staying long."

Old Cornelius nodded at me, gave Mary a stern look, and returned to his almanac.

"I'm fine," I said. "Go gossip with the ladies in town. I'll find you when I'm done."

I returned to my paper. It was almost complete, and I was sure it would turn out to be useful.

I was never going to break Gaucho. But maybe the key to working with someone, whether they're a person or a big bouncy bird, is to figure out where they're coming from. Whatever the case, I felt these might be the clues to my future. By the time I finally left with a disgruntled Mary and an Ernest who'd been waiting a full half hour longer than he'd bargained for, I didn't know what I had, but I knew it might come in handy.

1. Gaucho probably weighs 320 pounds, which is the same as two sheep.

2. He really does have eyeballs bigger than his brain (the Madame was right!)

3. Because his brain is so small, if a lion was coming to eat him, he'd probably run in a circle.

4. He can run forty miles an hour, which is twice as fast as a human.

5. If he kicked you, his toe claw could kill you by cutting you like a knife. But he can't kick backwards, so that's GOOD (?)

6. Some ostriches have blue necks. Not 'cause they're losing air or anything, though.

7. This part I don't get, but the air he breathes in isn't the air he breathes out? He can get fresh air even when he's breathing out stale air at the same time. So, basically, he can run without his lungs getting tired like ours do.

8. His legs are built for running. Half of Gaucho's weight is in his thighs, and his thighs are all muscle.

9. His backwards knee is actually his ankle (!?!) and his knee is way up his thigh. I definitely don't understand this, but pretty much his legs are just these enormous feet. Huh.

10. Ostriches don't sweat, they pant.

11. The average ostrich can live to be 75 years old.

Twenty

Naturally, it happened on the day my uncle wasn't there. And he was almost always there, but one afternoon my father told Uncle Fred in no uncertain terms that he was needed in the fields early the next day and that no matter what his job was at Madame Marantette's, it would have to wait for "real" work. Daddy was down two workers thanks to sickness and sunburn and needed to make up the manpower. "I suggested you come here so you could contribute to the farm, Fred. I haven't seen a penny from whatever it is you've been doing at that woman's house. So tomorrow, I'm sorry, but I need you with me."

Uncle Fred offered some weak protests of his own. It was

late July, the county fair only two weeks away. And great progress had been made with Gaucho and Bonnie Anne. Now they could pull the cart alongside each other, though neither was particularly good at finding the other's rhythm. You got the impression that Bonnie Anne was game, but trying to read the mind of an ostrich is like like reading the mind of a very, very intelligent potato. No matter your intentions, you're just not going to get all that far. The two had gotten proficient enough to pull Uncle Fred and Bud around once or twice, but the herky-jerky gait was still too rough for the Madame. Nevertheless, as the date of the fair grew nearer, her visits to the paddock had increased in frequency. She was spending more and more time observing and commenting on our efforts now. I admired how one swift, sure command from her could have an immediate effect on Gaucho and Bonnie Anne both. There was no denying who was in charge. I had surreptitiously watched her from afar for tips so that I could use them with Gaucho on my own. Today I was determined to put them to good use.

"Uncle Fred," I said as my father walked out of the room, "I can take over. I can do it. I've watched you long enough."

"How 'bout we both take a breather tomorrow, eh?"

"Uncle Fred, the parade's two weeks away!" I couldn't believe he needed this pointed out. "Gaucho needs all the practice he can get. And Bud will be there. We'll get Gaucho attached to the surrey, and I'll just take it slow, I promise. I won't try to break any records!"

Without a word, he simply nodded to me. I lit out of there in a blaze of happiness.

That night, I laid out my dresses. The grand total sum? Two. The calico was my regular churchgoing attire, light brown with little chocolate flowers spotted all around. But I had a fancier dress that came out when there were weddings or funerals to attend. A deep blue velvet affair, held at the waist by a blood-red silk ribbon, thick as an ostrich's neck. After some consideration, I figured the calico was good enough for the sidesaddle attempt. With Uncle Fred not present, I decided that tomorrow would be the ideal day to give it a trial run. Bud could help me wrangle Gaucho in place.

Long before the sun began to rise, I took off for the Madame's. The purple predawn light was just beginning to show when I arrived.

Bud was already working the farm animals when he saw me approach by myself.

"Is Fred not coming?" he asked.

"Nope," I said. "He has to work the fields today. But he said I could come in his place."

"Come in his place," repeated Bud.

"Come in his place to tend to Gaucho and hook him up with Bonnie Anne," I said, with more conviction than I felt.

Bud was having none of it. "No," he said. "This is your uncle's job and not yours. If the Madame wants to hire a man to train her ostrich, that's her business. But she didn't hire you. You're not strong enough to hitch. Also, if you get injured while tiring the ostrich, there's no one to shoulder the blame."

"I'll shoulder the blame myself," I said, but still he shook his head.

"That's not how blame works. If you're a kid, someone's going to point at the closest adult when you make stupid mistakes. And right now that someone is me. You," he said, pointing at me, "could get me killed, kid."

He seemed to mean that if I got on Gaucho and got hurt, then my family would blame him. Or maybe the Madame. Or maybe someone else. But I'd walked all the way there in my dress (which he hadn't even noticed, by the way), and I wasn't going to walk all the way back without trying at least one sidesaddle run. I decided to try another tactic. As Bud continued about the farm, I trailed after him like a puppy.

"Uncle Fred said you started working for the Madame in Europe."

"I did," he answered curtly.

"But you're not from there, you're from here, right?" I said. "So why were you in Europe?"

He got down the milking pail and approached a nearby cow. "Business," he said, clearly hoping to put me off.

I pulled up a stool beside him as he got to work. "What sort of business?"

He sighed. "I'm not going to get any work done until I answer you, am I?"

"None that I can see," I said brightly.

He reached into his breast pocket and pulled out a photo. Handing it to me, he said, "What do you see there?"

It was Bud, but a much younger Bud. He was wearing a skintight jacket of overlapping diamonds and standing proudly beside a horse. Around the horse's neck was a wreath with the words "Grand Prix de Deauville."

"Grand Pricks dee Dee-uv-vil," I recited solemnly. I looked up at him. "Did your horse win a race or something?"

He took the photo back, smiling. "He did. With me riding him the whole way. I was a jockey long before all of this. One of the best in the world, till an injury set me back and made it so I can't ride anymore." I recalled seeing him limp slightly but hadn't made much of it before. "Time was," he said, "that all the best jockeys were Black. And if you were slight and small like me, it was a way to get out and make good money," he explained. "My family's from Parkville. Farmers. Like yours. But I was always better with the horses than the land. Used to race them against other kids on nearby farms. We had a stretch of road we'd use going about a mile, and every other day I'd find someone to challenge there. And I won," he said smugly. "I always won."

"So you were like the Madame," I said. "You rode something and it got you out of town."

"That's the long and short of it," he said, soaping up the cow's udders. "Didn't take long for it to turn into a proper job.

A scout saw me racing once and snapped me up quick. Said goodbye to my family and soon I was racing in Kentucky with the best of them."

"Perfect!" I said.

"Not perfect." He stopped a moment and looked at me. "Michigan's not good to a Black man that makes money, but Kentucky's worse. So when the offer came to skip over to Europe, I took it. But the problem wasn't living there. It was getting back. After my injury I didn't want to leave, and then, after a while, I didn't have the money to anyway."

"And that's when you met up with the Madame."

"That's when." He cocked his head toward the house. "She took me on to tend the horses, and that's what I've mostly done since. Besides the odd farm chore," he said, indicating the cow. He smiled. "And now, apparently, babysitting."

He didn't say it mean, so I didn't take it that way. Just plunged forward. "So you got away from farming."

"I did," he said.

"I want to get away from farming," I said.

"Farming's not your problem, kid. You're a girl. Find yourself a husband and, depending on where he's bound, you could end up anywhere."

"I don't want to have to rely on anyone to take me away. I want to get away on my own."

"Well, that's a tricky business," said Bud, turning back to the cow. "Not many options out there."

"The Madame did it," I pointed out.

"The Madame is a high jump and racing champ," he countered. "She worked at it and got spotted at a county fair being the best there is. Not everyone can be the best."

"What if I become the best at riding an ostrich?" I asked. "What if I become a world-class ostrich rider?"

This amused him.

"What if"—and then I voiced something I'd never said before—"I'm an ostrich jumping champion?"

Bud burst into laughter. The cow shifted beside him, uncertain how to deal with all that mirth. Presently Bud calmed down, wiping his eyes with a handkerchief he kept in a pocket. "An ostrich jumper," he said. "That'll be the day. You ever see an ostrich jump?"

I shrugged. I didn't know it yet. I just surmised. "They've got knees," I said. "You've gotta have knees to jump."

"Yeah, well," he said, "caterpillars have knees too, but I don't see them going to championships anywhere."

"Can't ride a caterpillar," I said.

"You can barely ride an ostrich," he said.

"Look, I need your help. If you get Gaucho tacked up for me today, I'll ride him. I don't need Uncle Fred to ride, and you know I've got the grip." I flexed my fingers.

Bud didn't say anything for a couple minutes. Then he sighed. "All right," he said. "I'll get him set up for you. But I have other work to do. You can ride the bird, but you're not doing anything with Bonnie Anne or the surrey, understand?"

"Understood," I agreed. The Madame had told me that a farm girl on an ostrich was a novelty but a young lady on an ostrich was an event. I planned on being an event.

Twenty-One

I don't think there's an ostrich in this great green world that has heard the human voice half so much as Gaucho had in those past few weeks. Every time we trained, I'd bring the bag and we'd play "Who wants the baggy?" (answer: not the ostrich) for a while. I'd bag his head, then whip it off, and we'd run. I got the weird feeling that Gaucho was actually coming to like this game. When we opened the pasture doors now, he would separate himself from whatever it was he was doing and shimmy over. Sometimes it seemed like he'd been waiting for me. And we would run.

The joy that Gaucho felt while running, the joy the Madame had talked about to me before, I hadn't really understood it then. But the more we kept doing it together, the more it made sense. I thought about what I'd learned in the library. Technically he was physically built to run, with his strong thighs and lungs that could let him go without getting out of breath. A lot of the time, a wild ostrich runs to get away from something that scares it. What made Gaucho different from the other ostriches wasn't that he was meaner or anything (even if he was), but that when he ran, when he *really* ran, he did it because it made him happy. I think he knew somewhere that he was the fastest thing around when he ran. And maybe he was beginning to understand that if he stuck with me, we could run together.

After he'd gotten some energy out and was more docile, I'd try to make him understand words like "walk" and "forward" and "stop." Turns out "forward" and "stop" were words the Madame had taught him for pulling her surrey, so it didn't take much work for him to connect her commands and my own in his head.

Today was like any other. Gaucho was waiting for me when I arrived. He was the same. It was me who was different. Different and determined to do something new.

Bud slowly led Gaucho out from the pasture and into the paddock.

"No ladder today either? Not even with that dress you're wearing?"

I looked down on it. Somehow, before any of this had even begun, I'd already managed to get some mud on the hem. I scraped at it with my fingernail and shook my head. "No, no, I'm good here. Just lead him over."

Gaucho turned his head at the sound of my voice, but while me riding him around the pasture was familiar to him, coming into the paddock was not. I felt a little bad for him— I could see his thoughts ping-ponging around his itty-bitty headspace—but there was no help for it. Like it or not, the pasture had too much space for what I was planning today. I also didn't want the distracting presence of the other birds to upset Gaucho in this test run. He reared back a little ways, not certain what to do. Bud tightened his grip and talked calmly to the bird. "Easy now, easy now, there. That's just Suzy. She's going to ride you like always."

I should probably say that at this point I had not let Bud in on the whole sidesaddle plan. I won't lie. I was a little nervous, but I wasn't completely unprepared or anything. For the past week, I'd been having secret sidesaddle lessons. And by "lessons" I mean I'd been sidesaddle sitting on our old nag, Frances, and our mules, Clarke and Sayer, for practice. Now, Frances is half blind and hasn't so much as cantered since before Dotty was born. Clarke and Sayer, in contrast, are lazy, so getting them to do pretty much anything you want at all is not usually on the schedule. Add in the fact that I didn't own a sidesaddle (it's got special pommels and a stirrup so that it's harder to fall) and was doing all this riding bareback. Maybe I shouldn't have been quite so cocky about my chances.

But cocky I was, and I felt like I had a good reason to be. These last few weeks I'd felt a grudging respect for Gaucho, and I fancied he felt one for me. He knew my voice and my weight. Knew my routines and how they went. And it wasn't like I was intending to do something out of the ordinary. My plan was to get on, same as always, and then when Gaucho had gone through the usual paces, I'd swing a leg back over and try this sidesaddle business. Easy-peasy.

Gaucho allowed himself to be led closer to me, and taking the reins in my left hand, I shouted, "Up, up, Gaucho!" Then I took a little running leap and swung my leg over his back with what was now a swift, practiced movement.

"And we're off," said Bud, and he backed away.

Penned into the paddock with less space than the pasture, Gaucho still managed a madcap, wild ride back and forth. By this point I knew more of the tricks. How to tuck my legs beneath his wings. How to tug his neck and pull it one way or another if I wanted him not to crash into something. When Bud was confident I wasn't going to go plummeting, he excused himself, telling me to call him when Gaucho was plumb tired enough.

While I rode, I kept thinking about what the Madame had

said. "A true rider doesn't use her *knees* to maintain balance on a steed. Your power is in your grasp and poise, not the contortions of your lower extremities." The thing about ostrich riding is that it's not an elegant mode of travel. Ride a horse correctly and you look like a queen. Ride an ostrich correctly and your head is still going bobbity bobbity bobbity so fast you'd swear you were running on cobblestones. If I was going to do this sidesaddle and in a dress, then I needed to be smart about it. After the appropriate amount of time, Gaucho started to slow himself down. And so, before I could talk myself out of it, I swung my right leg over, settling it next to my left. There it was. When it came to riding Gaucho, the knees were no longer in the picture.

He felt it, of course. How could he not? And he waited a bit too. In his experience, if the legs were on the same side, then I was preparing to dismount. When I didn't, he padded about a bit, testing me. My hands were at the base of his neck, holding on for dear life, but I was careful not to squeeze. We circled the paddock once, twice, three times. The thickset brown-and-yellow mud of the paddock was far below me. I could see the pasture beyond, Gaucho's playmates looking over at what was, by now, a fairly regular display. The wind whipped out of the east, blowing the tall grasses of the adjoining farmland, scents of hot hay wafting in my direction. The sun-warmed sumac and the orchards lay far beyond.

My heart leapt in my chest. I was doing this! *We* were doing this. In that moment, Gaucho and I were compatriots, equals. Partners in an endeavor that could prove to be bigger than either of us. We understood one another in a way that no one else could. I was, in that moment, conquering the world with an impossible creature by my side.

Naturally, this was the same moment the fool bird decided to make a headlong leap for freedom.

It happened so fast there wasn't much I could have done to stop it. The next thing I knew, Gaucho was careening toward the side of the paddock. I reached up to grab the upper part of his neck to swerve him to the side, but I didn't realize that he was, at that moment, jumping.

It turns out that ostriches can actually jump. But Gaucho didn't quite clear the five-foot paddock gate, even though he stood at least nine feet tall. His big old horned feet got caught on the top board of the fence, causing his rider, and that would be me, to be thrown forward at a massive speed that far exceeded the piddly drops I'd experienced up until that point. I flew a good long way before landing, hard, on my shoulder.

The pain was excruciating, but that wasn't the best of it. Kicking and flapping for all he was worth, Gaucho managed to get himself the rest of the way over the fence, and when he realized he was now free, he took off running fast as I'd ever seen him, down the road, away from me, away from the Madame, to who knows where. Through the haze of pain popped up the unwelcome fact that ostriches can run forty miles an hour if they want to.

I heard the Madame somewhere behind me calling out, and Bud swearing. A moment later I felt myself being lifted up slightly, my whole body shuddering without my permission.

"Where do you hurt?" Bud asked gravely.

"My—my shoulder," I choked out after a few attempts.

He eyed it but made no move to touch it, for which I was grateful. "Does anything else hurt?"

My head was still spinning from the tumble but had mercifully avoided a blow. I had a sudden understanding of why it was that so many thrown riders died of broken necks. A slight maneuver in another direction and I would have been in the same sorry state. I shook my head. Bud just said, "Kid, you don't know how lucky you are." And I did but was unable to express it in any way.

"I will take her home," the Madame said. "Take one of the horses. St. Patrick, perhaps. See if you can't catch up with Gaucho. He could be anywhere by this point. I want him back alive."

Bud shook his head. "I can't promise that."

"Please try. Please." I heard a crack in her voice. A pause. Then, with no crack, "He means the world to me. He was Daniel's last present. Please, Bud."

Bud sighed and picked me up, taking care to avoid my hurt shoulder. He carried me to the wagon, placed me in the front, and then said, "I'll see what I can do."

He draped a quilt of some sort across my shoulders. Then the Madame hitched up Bonnie Anne and sat herself beside me, taking me home like a booby prize my parents would have no wish to collect. With every clatter of the wagon, my hurt shoulder was jostled and I moaned in pain.

The Madame glanced over to me from time to time, but these looks were less concerned than they were appraising. After a while she said, "Your first injury. And not the ribs either. Probably just a dislocated shoulder, but the doctors will know for sure. There is, as you can now see, no gain without a fair amount of pain."

I was in no position to do much more than glare at her, though I did manage to say between gritted teeth, "I wouldn't have fallen if I hadn't been riding sidesaddle."

She nodded, as if she'd known all along, and I suppose she had. "It is as I told you. Sidesaddle is the more difficult art. All attempts at true virtue are."

We said no more after that. There really wasn't all that much more to say.

Twenty-Two

Daddy was going to be angry at me. Daddy had never really been angry at me before, and the idea of finding myself on the receiving end of his cold, clear fury was worse, much worse, than the shoulder I clutched as we approached the house. All through Burr Oak, people had torn out of their homes to see the Madame, her back ramrod straight, directing her cart to my home. When we pulled in, someone must have alerted my parents, because it looked like everyone and their brother was there to greet me. Even the chickens looked like they were on high alert. As we neared, I noticed how they walked and it made me think about Gaucho's funny gait. Where was he now?

Daddy, meanwhile, was raging. Not the way most men do with their swears and cries and violent fists. The way Daddy did it was all quiet. A simmering sea beneath the surface that made everything around him cold and still. He looked at me. Just looked, and it was worse than thirty of Granny's switches. I just about died on the spot.

The Madame stood in the wagon, and I swore she could have been about ten feet tall, the way she looked down.

"What happened to my daughter?" Daddy demanded.

The Madame flicked her eyes at me and flicked 'em back. "She appears to have a dislocated shoulder from a fall. She was riding Gaucho, and he decided to make an attempt at jumping the fence. She was thrown. Could have happened to any rider."

"*Could* have happened," said my father, "but it *actually* happened to my child." He swung his eyes over to Uncle Fred. "This is what she's been doing the whole time she's been over there? I thought you had her doing odd jobs or chores or something . . . something safe! Instead you've been having her riding unbroken horses?"

"It wasn't a horse she was riding. It was an ostrich," the Madame said coldly.

It took a second for that one to sink in. Daddy stared at her.

"An ostrich," he repeated dully.

"An ostrich," she agreed.

"An ostrich." It seemed like the word could not be said enough.

Suddenly a ridiculous grin cracked open all over Daddy's face. He started laughing like it was the funniest thing he'd ever heard. "Do you mean to say," he gasped, when he was able to get some feeling back, "that Suzy has been ostrich riding?"

The Madame didn't like being laughed at. Nobody does. But her way of responding to it was to up the dignity quotient even higher. Her voice fell a full octave. "She has," she replied.

That just made Daddy hoot even more, and in a moment the whole yard was full of other hooting relatives. It was like they were telling the story of my birth or something. I was having a real hard time deciding if this made me mad or not. The agony in my shoulder intense, I called out, "Mama?"

I could tell a battle was raging in my mama beneath the surface. The idea of an everyday horse accident turning out to be ostrich-related instead was throwing her for a bit of a loop. But the pain of her child overwhelmed the ridiculousness of the situation, and she pushed through. "Of course,

of course," she murmured. "Come inside and we'll call Dr. Royer." And in we went without so much as a by-your-leave to the Madame.

☆☆☆

My days of misery went from awful to great to downright terrible. Awful because when Doc Royer arrived he agreed with the Madame's assessment about it being a dislocated shoulder and lost no time in setting it right. Setting it turned out to hurt worse than the dislocation itself, but the immediate relief was worth it. Then all the family members, even Granny to a certain extent (which is to say, she didn't switch me), were fawning over me, giving me get-well presents and the like. Except Bill, of course. He kept offering to punch my injured shoulder to make sure it was healing right. I told him one neat punch and I'd say it was dislocated again and direct Daddy on who was to blame. He left me alone after that.

What I hadn't really counted on were the downright terrible aspects that came after that. Uncle Fred came to see me. He had his hat in hand, which, for some reason or another, struck me as sad. He knocked real soft, and when I said he could come in, he stood in the doorway for a minute or two, blinking, turning the brim of his hat around in his hands, over and over and over. Then, silently, he shuffled in, closed the door, and took a seat next to my bed.

Ten full minutes passed before he said a word. I almost couldn't make it out when he did, and when I understood him, I wished I hadn't.

"Never should have let you come."

I lay there, looking at him.

"The minute I knowed you were following me . . . should have turned right around then."

"Why didn't you?" I asked.

His eyes were real shiny. Kept blinking them. "Didn't want to," he said after a spell. "It's been a long time since someone actually wanted . . . that someone walked with me." He looked over and worked up one of those smiles that didn't touch his eyes. "You're good company."

"You too," I said softly.

His eyes met mine, then flicked over to the bandages holding my shoulder in place. His bent back straightened as he came to a decision, and even as I lay there watching it happen, I knew that there was nothing I could do to stop it.

"I'm not taking you back there, Suzy."

"Not much of a point," I conceded. "Doc says my shoulder shouldn't get any more bumps for a while. It's sore, but I can still use it, so when we take Gaucho to the fair . . ."

I stopped. Gaucho! In all that was going on with me, I'd plumb forgotten my ostrich. "Hey! Wait! What happened? Is he okay? Did Bud . . . ?"

"Funny you should worry about the one that did this to you and not yourself." Uncle Fred was frowning now, and I didn't like the look on him one bit, but I couldn't stop pestering him.

"Please. Uncle Fred, did they get Gaucho back?"

"Yeah, they got him back. . . ."

"And is he safe? Did they get him back . . . y'know . . . alive?" That last word came out more like a little chirp in the back of my throat. I had sudden visions of Gaucho in my mind, hurt and scared, somewhere strange. I envisioned him mauled by a bull or torn to shreds by a pack of bloodhounds. Worse, I could easily see him shot by one of our neighbors, just for the thrill of bagging something that big.

Uncle Fred didn't want to answer me, I could see it. But I wasn't acting when my own eyes got shiny. Shinier than his own even. He let out this big old exasperated puff of air and said, "He's fine. Bud got him with the help of some of the men in town. Not before the bird got a good kick at Orla Richards in the midsection. But I think Doc Royer said the cuts weren't that deep."

"Did Bud get hurt?" I asked, concerned. I remembered reading about that toe claw ostriches have. How it's sharp as a blade and can disembowel a lion in seconds.

He nodded. "Mostly cut up his clothing, though. A couple cuts to the legs, nothing that required stitches, but he told the Madame that he is definitely not working with 'that ostrich' anymore. I guess it's on just me now, though I dunno how I can do it alone for just half a day. They've got Gaucho back in the pasture in any case."

"Then I'll go see him when they let me out of bed," I said resolutely.

"No, Suzy. You won't!" This was said with more force than I'd heard come out of Uncle Fred's mouth since the moment I'd made his acquaintance.

"Of course I will! I've gotta see—"

"Are you even hearing me?" My uncle looked at me like I was growing a second head. "Did you hear what I said just a minute ago? I'm not taking you back there again. I shouldn't have done it from the start, and I definitely shouldn't have let you get near, let alone ride, that devil of an ostrich! You're never going back, Suzy! You could have broken your neck and never been able to walk again. You could have . . ." He choked off.

"But I didn't, Uncle Fred! Look at me! I'm fine!"

"You're not fine. You've got your whole big, beautiful life ahead of you, and I'm not gonna be the one who stops you from living it." He crumpled his hat in his hands and stormed out of the room.

That was the first terrible thing that happened.

The second terrible thing was that a week before the St. Joseph County Fair, Daddy and Mama were united in informing me that I was not going.

"WHAT?!" I don't think I'd ever shrieked under our roof a day of my life, but I was shrieking then. "But, but, but . . ." I sputtered for a while and then found my words. "But that's when the parade is."

"Parades come and go, sweetheart," said Mama, all sympathetic eyes and iron resolve. "But you've got to know sneaking off to ride horses or ostriches or what have you isn't something we countenance."

I managed to prevent myself from speaking purely in

shrieks. "But at the parade, the Madame will be driving Bonnie Anne and Gaucho!"

They blinked at me uncomprehendingly.

"She's going to break a world record for having a horse and an ostrich pulling a surrey together for the first time!"

Daddy frowned. "How can you have a world record for something that's never existed before?"

I didn't have an answer to that and I didn't need to. "Daddy," I insisted. "I'll never ask for anything else in my life. But I have to see that parade. I have to see Gaucho run."

"That fool ostrich that threw you down in the first place?" I could see the ire rising in Daddy's face before I could stop it. The funny part of that story had faded away long since in the wake of the doctor's visit. "No, Suzy, you will NOT be seeing it again. You will not be seeing it unless there's some way I can find to brine and bind that bird for our Sunday supper!" And then he slammed his way out, as mad as a wet hen. Madder.

Mama watched him leave. "Please, Mama," I said in vain. She sighed and gently pushed me down to the bed. "You rest now, sweetheart. It'll all seem better in the morning."

I lay there, eyes wide. It might seem better at that. But "seems" and "is" are two different matters separated by a canyon or more. Plus, a new thought had crawled into my brain to take root and keep me from my sleep. My family had never seen me ride Gaucho. Just Uncle Fred, and I was beginning to understand how little that counted. I had to get out of Burr Oak, and if I looked at it from just the right angle, Gaucho was the one to take me away. Because the only way I was going to break free of my tiny town and my tinier family was to show them I was capable of something brighter and bigger.

A plan began to congeal in my sleep-deprived head.

☆☆☆

I have always been of the mindset that when you need a tool for a job, you find the best tool. And if that tool happens to be a despicable genius of chaos, then you find yourself that genius. So that's how my brother Bill found himself with a visitor in the early hours of the morning the next day.

"Huhhhnn . . . wha—?" he exclaimed sleepily. "Wait . . . Suzy?" he said, scrambling a bit away from me and to the wall. Like I was gonna hurt him. Like I couldn't have done it long before then anyway.

I leaned in close. "Listen, Bill. My arm's in a sling." I indicated the arm. "I've got a real problem here and I need your help."

He rubbed the sleep from his eyes and settled them into

a comfortable, customary glare. "What do you need 'my help' for? Nobody needs my help."

"I do," I insisted. The night before I'd worked it all out. And in the course of things I thought I'd worked out Bill too. He was still the boy with something wrong in his head, that was for sure and for certain. But at the same time, I realized, nobody was taking that away from him. He was treated like an outcast, and so an outcast he'd continue to become. And unless someone started counting on him to do something right real soon, he was gonna keep on doing wrong until the end of his livelong days. Sure, my method of drawing him to the truth and the light was going to involve breaking our parents' hearts a little, to say nothing of their rules, but as far as I was concerned, the ends justified the means. And maybe Bill would agree.

Before he could sputter another syllable, I told him about my plan. And along the way I told him a lot of other stuff too. About the Madame and her coming back to her hometown, even when everyone she loved there was gone. About Bud and his amazing life that had brought him to the Madame's farm, not so far from where he'd begun. And about me and what I wanted. How I might leave, travel the world, and end up back here someday, maybe, but maybe not. Maybe I'd end up somewhere else. And how that was okay too. 'Cause wild as it seemed, out of all my siblings, Bill was the only one who paid enough attention to me that he'd figured out my dreams.

Bill sat there in silence. I don't think I'd ever seen him sit so long and listen so well for anyone. Not for the teachers in school, certainly. One of them had gone so far as to name his ruler "Bill" in honor of its most frequent victim. And our parents weren't real talkers, so he'd never really listened to them. Only once in a while when Mama was reciting one of her stories from memory, like the *Tom Sawyer* chapter about whitewashing the fence, would he listen like this, quiet as a church mouse. Serious as a grave.

"Why we doing this?" he asked.

I stopped. I thought I'd covered all of that.

"For yourself," he answered. "You've got it all tangled up together with those other stories. Admit it. Admit that you're doing this for yourself."

"Why?" Seemed like a reasonable question.

"Because you're asking me to help you do something you think can get you away from here. And how? You just told me the Madame's retired. She can't do anything for you now. So what's this gonna prove to anyone? Why"—he put his finger down hard on the quilt between us—"do I put myself on the line so that you can break the rules, rub them in Mama's and Daddy's faces, and then I get nothing out of it?"

"Because maybe it'll work," I said. "Maybe a miracle will

happen. Maybe a scout will be there. Maybe the Madame will write me a magic letter and get me a circus job. Or maybe nothing, but I've gotta try, don't I?" I looked at him hard. "I gotta try."

"And I help you because . . . ?"

"Because it'll make Mama and Daddy bonkers."

He snorted. "I don't need you for that."

He was right. So what did I have to offer him that he didn't already have?

And then it came to me. Like a bolt from the blue. It took less than a second to sit right there on the quilt and make a decision. I offered him something that no one else could, and he listened. Listened so hard it looked like his ears might turn purple with the strain.

I offered him his heart's desire.

When I was done, a second or two passed, and then he nodded curtly and held out his hand. We shook on it.

"I'm in. Now. How we gonna do this?"

Twenty-Three

The day of the St. Joseph County Fair parade, the sky bloomed bright and blue and merry. And while most of us had winter finery and church finery, county fair finery was a bit different. It was billowing summer dresses and short-sleeved shirts. Button-up knickers and hair in braids. Everyone in my family was dressed to the nines. Everyone, that is, except for me and Granny.

I sat, bereft, at the breakfast table, while around me my siblings and parents and relatives all primped and primed. Mary, who had taken a shine to Aunt Juliet, was wetting our aunt's hair then doing it in straight braids on either side of her head. When she finished, Aunt Juliet almost smiled. Almost.

Dotty was wearing a dress that twirled almost as much as she did when she spun, and Bill was being obnoxious to me. The difference was, I didn't mind a bit and even admired him for the act. If he really and truly was going to help me out that day, it only made sense that he'd be a jerk to me so as not to arouse any suspicions.

"Suzy's not going to the pa-rade, Suzy's not going to the pa-rade," he chanted merrily.

I let out a wail of "Mama!" and she leapt to my defense, saying, "One more word out of you, young man, and you won't be going to the parade either." That shut him up right quick, and when Mama's back was turned he gave me a wink. I winked back. It was odd to be on the same side as him, but also weirdly thrilling. If today went right, I'd be just as mistrusted as ever he had been. But maybe, just maybe, it'd be worth it.

Uncle Fred was one of the few people at the table not looking his level best. Sure, he'd spruced up a jot. I think he'd even washed his hands with soap at one point, though the grime was so seeped into the cracks and fissures of his fingers that nothing short of lye could have burned that dirt away. On occasion he'd cast his woebegone puppy-dog eyes in my direction in a kind of silent supplication for forgiveness, and I'd try to shoot him a winning smile in response. I thought that might alleviate his guilt, but every time I tried it, he just sighed harder and turned back to the scrambled eggs before him. I couldn't really blame him. They were excellent scrambled eggs. I'd had a mess of them already myself (worm-free).

For my part, I was just ready for my family to get out and get moving. And, in the course of things, they finally did. Except Granny. It was decided that she would be the one to stay home with me to keep me in line. No escape. No way out. Granny and I waved morosely from the front porch while the whole cart of relatives took off, and I caught Bill's eye. He gave me a subtle thumbs-up to indicate that everything would turn out all right. I hoped it was true, though I could see all kinds of holes in the plan we'd constructed. Had we thought of everything? Was there some detail we'd overlooked? Miscalculated? Underestimated? Too late now. The minute the wagon was out of sight the clock was officially ticking.

When the cart was gone, Granny whupped me with a wooden spoon. "OW!" I cried. I rubbed the tender part of my scalp where her spoon of justice had made contact. "What was that for?"

"That, my dear, was for making me miss the fair today." She sniffed extravagantly. "And I was so looking forward to the peach ice cream." We walked into the house and I rolled my eyes behind her back. Granny hated the fair. Every year we went she insisted on going along as well, and then she spent the better part of five hours complaining about the following things in various forms of rotation: what the heat was doing to her hair, the number of people out, the dust, how today's crop of children was significantly louder than in past generations, the low-grade food, the bathrooms, Bill's behavior, our behavior, the behavior of our generation, and even the behavior of the president. Apparently, he was the one most to blame. The day I saw her with a happy little ice cream in hand would be the day I dived into Lake Michigan and swam myself to the Atlantic.

The next bit was tricky. It required a bit of acting on my part, and acting was never my strong suit when it came to Granny. So I put myself into the mind of a Suzy who might not have a plan for the day. What if I really was going to miss the parade? How would I feel? When Granny hobbled back into the foyer a moment later, I was lying on the couch, looking listlessly ahead.

"What's wrong with you?" she asked, giving my leg a thick thwap for good measure.

I didn't even twitch. "I don't feel so good."

"Bah. That's just petulance," she said. "You're feeling sorry for yourself because you didn't get to do the thing you wanted because of the bad thing you did. You'll find no pity in me." She spoke that last line with a certain amount of pride.

"May I go to my room, Granny?"

"Hmmph." She thought about that one, and I held my breath. Granny was very much of the old Children Should Be Seen and Not Heard camp. Only her version, Children Should Not Be Seen or Be Heard, was far preferable. I was now offering her this option, and if she took it, she might get a whole day to herself.

Just to test the waters out, Granny slammed her cane beside me with a resounding *WHACK*. I watched the puff of dust climb up and up from the spot on the love seat where the cane had landed, but I commanded myself not to flinch. Not so much as an eyelid. Not even a twitch to the brow.

Granny noted my general blah-ness and dismissed me. "Fine, then. Go. To your room. But don't expect any food unless you regain a willingness to work." I didn't need to be told twice. I dragged myself up the stairs to my room, where I made a quick change to my clothing.

I didn't have to wait long.

One short knock and three long ones at the window later, I leapt to the end of the room and threw open the sash. There, perched in a poplar tree, a grin stretched wide across his face, was my no-good, rotten brother.

"Did you have any trouble?" I asked as I raised the window for him.

According to the plan, Bill had to slip out of the cart unnoticed not long after leaving the farm. This was, I knew, the

crux of everything. If he got out too soon and they noticed, they'd just turn around and head back home to fetch him. If, however, they didn't notice until too late, they'd just figure he was being his own peculiar self (I mean, nobody runs *away* from the fair) and give a silent sigh of relief that they wouldn't have to deal with him for a couple hours.

"Nope." He climbed in, easy as a cat. "No one looks for me if I'm not causing trouble. They might not notice I'm gone till they get there. Or," he said glumly, "till it's time to go home. 'Cept Dotty, of course. She noticed right away when I slipped out, but she won't tell on me."

I agreed. "Not her. She thinks you're as nice as Granny."

Bill actually barked a little laugh at that, so's I had to shush him.

"And the rest of them probably won't have you on their minds when they're leaving," I reminded him.

He smirked. "I'm not doing this for free. I'm missing a whole day of judging competitions for you, y'know. You sure you can guarantee it's worth it?"

I remembered what I had promised him, and my heart sank. The Madame's words came to me. Something about sacrificing something to get what I wanted.

"The Madame needs people to take care of her ostriches. Bud doesn't want to do it, and Uncle Fred needs someone to do it with him. And he won't take me back to the farm anymore, so . . . so you go with him now." I glared at the floor and muttered, "You like working with animals. It fits. And Daddy will let you if you make a salary. I'll talk to the Madame and vouch for you."

The words sank deep into my soul. Bill. My worst enemy. And now he would get to go to the Madame's every day without me. He'd get to see Gaucho all the time. He'd get to take care of him and feed him and talk to the Madame. And me? I'd be back here in a house with Granny and probably even more chores to do, once my family had found out that I'd misled them for weeks.

Convincing Bill to stay home today had come with a steep price. I was gambling that it would be worth it in the end. But it was highly probable that I'd just handed the best thing I had going on in my life over to him.

Even so, I'd been surprised when he'd agreed to the deal. Considering how often I was the focus of his nastiness, I'd half figured he'd say no just to spite me. And yet, ever so slowly, I was now formulating a theory that maybe Bill was lonely. Maybe that was why he spent most of his time with creatures that couldn't yell or scream at him.

Or, more likely, maybe he knew the fair wouldn't be much fun anyway, since Daddy never let him run around or explore the livestock stalls for fear of the pranks he might pull.

I pulled back the quilt on my bed. "Go on. Get in."

He smirked but did as I said. "It's gonna be so strange, not being the worst kid for a while," he said. "I don't know what I'll do with myself."

"Try being nice," I said, and tucked the edges down around his ears. "Maybe it'll take."

"Wouldn't count on it," said his muffled voice.

Minutes later, I was scurrying out the window. My hurt shoulder growled at me as I worked my way out and down to the ground, but it wasn't too bad. I then got nice and close to the house so that Granny wouldn't see me if she happened to pop her head out this way. Quiet as a church mouse, I made my way to the barn, where I knew I could find Mary's pride and joy. The one thing she would never want me to touch on this or any day.

Her bicycle.

The bike had been an extravagant present from one of Mary's better-off boyfriends. I think he'd taken it into his mind that it could act as a kind of pre-dowry present to show his pure intent. Instead, Daddy had taken one look at the contraption and run the fellow out of town on a rail. Mary had wailed at the treatment, but secretly I think she was relieved at not being beholden to that rich boy's silly ways. The bike wasn't a pretty thing, but it was Mary's, and she made no bones about declaring it as such. I'd ridden it here and there a couple times, but it was so rickety around the gears that most of us had taken to calling it Old Boneshaker and left it at that.

Now, of all times, I needed its shaky ways. Trying my best to not get grease on any part of my personage, I lifted Boneshaker down from the wall and placed it on the ground. I swear the old right pedal leapt out and kicked me in the shin before I was ready to react. I glared double hard at it in vengeance, then flung a leg over its side. The act made my muscles remember Gaucho and how much I preferred riding him. When the bike failed to cause me any more physical pain, I chalked that up as a win, and we pushed off down the road. Straight on till Centreville.

Twenty-Four

A good bike and a strong leg can get you from Burr Oak to Centreville in about an hour. I had a crochety bike and a small leg, so my journey took me just a bit longer. Still and all, it wasn't hard to find. Along the way, I encountered cars and carts and carriages and surreys galore, every last one headed the same way as myself. The fair was the to-do of the summer, and no one seemed inclined to miss it. I was careful. My arm didn't hurt so much, but I had to do everything I could to avoid injury. At least until I got there. At least until I could find the Madame and Uncle Fred.

At last the fairgrounds appeared up ahead. I straightened my handlebars and gently curved my way through the gates. Everywhere there was something to see. Livestock of all shapes of sizes, and foods for the taking. There were vendors and clowns, singers and musicians. I stood there in a daze until I remembered the lumbering piece of metal I still clutched in my hands. Looking about, I located a large tree near the start of the gate. A number of other bicycles had been abandoned willy-nilly at its base. I just had to hope that no one took Mary's home as some kind of twisted concession prize at the end of the day.

It turned out that velvet was hot. Hot velvet made me sweat. Sweat and velvet didn't look so good together, and then when the dust of the road clung and congealed to the sweaty parts of the velvet, the result was a bit sticky, a bit muddy, a bit smelly, and not at all the good impression I was hoping for.

I snaked, dived, and pushed to make my way to the front of the crowd at the start of the parade route. I had somewhere to be, and by gum I wasn't going to miss it for all the fishies in the sea. Thankfully, none of my family members were in sight. Luck was with me. They must've been a farther ways down.

The parade marshal, dressed in the floppiest, ugliest hat I'd ever seen, walked down the center of the street. As he passed me, he opened his little rosebud of a mouth.

"MAKE WAY! MAKE WAY! THE ANNUAL ST. JOSEPH COUNTY FAIR DAY PARADE IS BEGINNING! HOLD ON TO

YOUR HATS FOR THE GREAT MADAME MARANTETTE
AND HER LATEST WORLD RECORD ATTEMPT! MAKE
WAY! MAKE WAY!"

Finally he stood off to one side, and we beheld her at last.

The Madame was seated in a low cart without back or
top or sides. At the front stood Gaucho and Bonnie Anne,
neither taking so much as a step before she gave them the go-
ahead. Upon seeing her, the crowds went wild, applauding as
though their hands depended on it. The Madame settled into
that applause like a woman putting on a fine fur coat. It nes-
tled down around her so naturally that, for a moment, I had
a hard time recollecting what she looked like without it. She
was a woman in her element again. One who had spent the
better part of her life in front of large crowds of people, willing herself to defy expectations and do the impossible. And
seventy-year-old women do not usually break world records.

She wore her riding hat today. A smaller affair than those
large plumed ones she usually favored. At the base of her
throat, glinting in the sun, was the silver brooch of a horse
and rider. She surveyed the crowd, then nodded to Uncle
Fred, who removed Gaucho's bag, and with a flick of the Madame's wrists, Bonnie Anne began to walk.

I held my breath. Bonnie Anne had moved forward a
couple paces, drawing the surrey too far in one direction, before Gaucho got the hint. He started walking as well, possibly

hoping to surge past the horse at his side, but the Madame pulled back on his reins and brought the two together. She'd been a horsewoman longer than most of us had been alive, after all, and a racer before she was a jumper. The two started at a trot, and then increased to a canter. As they passed, the people hooted and waved with the sheer delight of witnessing history. Never once did so much as a vertebra on the Madame's back curve or change. She was like a statue. The essence of poise itself.

I hadn't seen Gaucho since the day he'd thrown me, and watching him now, I felt a surge of pride. *Look at him!* I thought back to when I'd first seen him paired with Bonnie Anne, and how the two had spent a goodly amount of time and energy trying to get away from one another. Now he was matching her stride as well as his two legs were able.

As they passed, I thought I saw the Madame's head incline just the smallest millimeter in my direction, but it could have been a fluke. In any case, I wasted no time. Gathering up my skirts, I ducked back and ran alongside the parade route to its end. I didn't know how long it would take the Madame to stop. All I knew was that when she did, I had to be there.

At one point I thought I spotted my sister, the belle of the fair, surrounded by handsome young men, but I had no seconds to waste. The parade ended around the corner of another building, and by the time I arrived, Bud was on the other end, already helping the Madame off the surrey. The customary bag was on Gaucho's head, but he didn't look tired or winded.

I marched right up to them, and the Madame gave me a rare smile.

"Did you see it, then?" she asked. Still out of breath myself, I just nodded. She nodded back. "A feat that will never be matched, I assure you."

"Congratulations," I gasped. Then, still before I had enough of my air, I said, "I want to ride Gaucho."

The Madame stopped cold.

"What did you say?"

"I said . . . I want to ride . . . Gaucho." I stood up more. Made full eye contact then and folded my hands before me.

The Madame looked at Bud. He

wasn't smiling, but his eyes were dancing. He knew perfectly well that something was going on. I hoped I'd guessed right about this.

She turned away from me then and began removing some of the tack from Bonnie Anne. "And why should I allow you to do this?" she asked quietly.

I steadied myself. "You told me once that to be successful, the one thing I needed was pure dogged tenacity," I said. "You said I shouldn't give up when people say no. Well, I'm not giving up. And I want to ride Gaucho."

She weighed what I'd said. "There's a second part to that advice," she murmured at last. "And it is this: Tenacity will get you far, but that's only if you make smart choices in what you strive for. The rider who doesn't know when to let go and leap off the horse is the rider who is ultimately crushed by her mount. You grip hard. But do you know when to let go?"

I looked at her. "I can let go," I said after a while. "But only if I'm getting thrown off." Looked her dead in the eye. "I'm not getting thrown off right now."

We held each other's gazes in that moment.

"Well, then," she said. "You'd better get your steed in position." And she smiled at me wide and proud.

I'd passed. But it wasn't over yet.

The next thing to do was to get Gaucho back to the start of the parade route, and that meant walking him through the crowds. This was no small job, since the route was packed with people, and Gaucho wasn't so much as what you'd call a friendly bird. I did my best to distract him by chattering nonstop as we walked.

"That smell you got there? That's the popcorn vendor, and that other smell is the one making all those elephant ears covered with cinnamon and sugar I love so much. Now we're getting around a nice big family of, well, what looks like seventy million small children, so watch your feet, Gaucho. Don't want you to squash a tot. Now we're just gonna go around . . . okay, apparently we're gonna go over that log they put out for sitting on. You don't have to go forward no matter what, you silly bird. And now we're approaching Mimi . . . Mimi!"

Dead smack ahead of us stood my best friend, her face red in the hot summer sun, a vanilla ice cream melting in her hand. She looked from me to the bird and back again in astonishment.

"Suzy! I thought you were still in bed with ten broken bones and a head injury besides?"

I laughed. "Is that what the rumor mill is saying? Naw, Mimi, I just got a dislocated shoulder from my . . . Oh! Lemme introduce you!" I pulled on Gaucho's reins so that his covered head was level with my friend's. "Mimi, Gaucho. Gaucho, Mimi."

"Charmed!" said Mimi loftily.

"I'd offer to have you meet officially, but I think he'd eat that ice cream out of your hand. Right after he ate your hat."

"Well, it is a delicious hat," she conceded. "Only the finest straw. But what are you doing leading the Madame's bird the wrong way along the parade route? I'd have thought you'd be sitting with your family over there." And she pointed to an area not far off, where what I saw made me feel all cold on that steaming-hot day.

The whole clan of them were sitting up ahead of me, off to the side on the grass, eating watermelon and cold ices.

"Mimi!" I hissed. "You've gotta help me! They think I'm home locked in my room, with Granny guarding the door!"

Mimi immediately understood the situation but was as stumped as I was to figure out how to sneak past. "What if . . . ," she said, grasping at straws. "What if you were to, I dunno . . . ride him past?"

"Mimi, how's that supposed to work? If they're likely to notice me when I'm *not* sitting on the ostrich, I think they're gonna notice me when I'm way up on top of it."

"I know, I know," she said, but she was clearly warming to the idea. "But . . . come on! Just try it!" And before I could stop her, she had whipped the bag off of Gaucho's head.

Time froze.

Naturally, that was the moment I heard my name.

"Suzy?" I heard my mother's gasp and turned to find her approaching at top speed. Gaucho could have learned a thing or two from her. "What on earth are you doing here? In that dress? With that . . ." She took in the bird beside me and gasped anew. "Is that the bird that tried to kill you?"

Before I could even answer, my father had come up behind her. "Here," he said, reaching for the reins in my hand. "I'll take that from you."

Gaucho had remained stock-still when the bag was removed, possibly allowing his eyes to readjust to the sunlight, but I knew my time was almost out. We were mere seconds away from a rampaging ostrich. If he killed or maimed anyone, the Madame's new record would be a mere side note alongside national news articles about how a perfectly quaint small-town parade turned into a scene of bloodshed and horror thanks to the foolish bumbling of a twelve-year-old girl.

"Up, up, Gaucho!" I shouted at him, then took a leap and pulled myself onto his back.

I had forgotten about my shoulder. My muscles screamed in protest, and I think I screamed a little too. Still and all, my hands stayed clamped tight, and with more flailing and flashing of my bloomers than was strictly decent, I got right up on top of him.

Taking his reins, I shied away from both my parents, forcing Gaucho to stumble a bit to the side. "Mama, Daddy," I said, as calmly as I was able through pain-gritted teeth, "I have to do this. You can punish me all you want afterwards, but this is something I gotta do." I thought about saying "please," then realized that there was sometimes something stronger than "please" in this world. I was doing this for me, sure. But in truth, half of it was for them. I needed them to see. "Now."

Then I saw Uncle Fred. He was on his feet beside my brother Ernest and my sisters and what now looked like half the southwest corner of the state as crowds of people gawked around me. Of all the people here, Uncle Fred knew the danger we were in as well as I. He saw Mimi and cried, "Get that bag back onto his head!"

The first time I'd ever tried to bag Gaucho, I'd had to do it from his back. Mimi, however, was a farm girl like me. She knew how livestock operated, and she knew that when necessity calls, you cannot wait for permission. With a strength that I admired and envied in turn, Mimi took hold of Gaucho's neck, pulled down his head, and popped the bag on right quick.

I took that to be my excuse to leave. "Look for me at the end of the parade!" I called, directing Gaucho forward so that the crowd had to part to let him through.

I heard a lot of spluttering from my parents behind me, a cheer from Mimi and a couple of other people, and even a "Go get 'em, Suzy!" from what sounded like Uncle Fred. I glanced back and saw that for the first time since I'd met him, he was smiling. Really and truly smiling. All the way up to his eyes and back.

After that, Gaucho and I practically ran to the parade start.

There wasn't much going on there. The stragglers were still waiting their turn to go. It was mostly some politicians and, finally, the mayor, sitting in an open-air tin lizzie with a sign reading "Mayor of Centreville" plastered to the side of the car.

In one of the Madame's lessons in comportment, she'd mentioned to me that establishing a good first impression is often the key to your future success. "When you meet royalty, Suzy, your impression must be a fine combination of both deference and the understanding that you too are a person worthy of respect." I did not, at the time, want to point out to her that the chance of my mingling with the kings and queens of Europe was about as likely as that of Gaucho learning to dance the turkey trot. But now I realized there might be a method to her madness. The mayor of Centreville was no king, but in this moment, I determined to pretend otherwise.

Murmuring sweet nothings to Gaucho, I managed to swing one of my legs up and over his side and settle there. I was once more a sidesaddle rider. In place, I took a chance and removed the bag.

Fortunately, what I had under my legs was one tuckered bit of overstuffed poultry. He'd been ridden by Uncle Fred early that morning, pulled the Madame, and walked a whole parade route back with me. When I urged him forward toward the mayor, he could have flapped and run some more, but he didn't. He walked calmly forward, and when I pulled back, he stopped.

There was one more piece of luck on my side that I didn't learn until later. Turns out, the mayor of Centreville was frightened to death of chickens. He probably didn't even know that that extended to ostriches as well until that very day.

Lucky me.

"Mr. Mayor," I said. I wondered if I should be lowering my voice like the Madame but worried it would sound like I was trying to imitate a bullfrog. So, instead, I just said, all matter-of-fact, "I'll be riding in front of you at the end of the parade."

He blinked up at me several times very quickly, and I saw five little nodules of sweat pop out, all at the same time. "Young lady, are you quite safe up there?"

Posture, said the Madame's voice in my head. *Throw back your shoulders and feel your spine settle into place.* I sat up, rearranged my skirts, and said, cool as a cucumber, "I'm quite all right, sir. So is Gaucho. We'll get into position."

The Madame said that if you don't ask permission and

just do something like it's already a done deal, often people will let you get away with it. That's not a lesson I wanted my mama and daddy to know that I'd learned, but it was one of the most useful things the Madame ever taught me. Because just like that, it was arranged. The increasingly sweaty mayor waved me to the front of his car, and we stood there, ready.

I put the bag back onto Gaucho's head while we waited to go and then worked on maintaining my posture while making some vows.

Someday I'd get permission to go back to the Madame's farm. My parents would have a devil of a time keeping me away after this. I would teach Gaucho to jump on purpose. Not fences yet, but little things. We'd work our way up. Get him to jump higher and higher, with me sitting on him all the while. There was not, as far as I knew, an ostrich high jump record for sidesaddle quite yet.

I increased my grip. Gaucho was ready to take off, and I was going to hold on while he took me wherever I wanted to go.

Epilogue

Ten years later . . .

The death announcement appeared in more than just the local papers. National news and even a couple of international organizations picked up on the story. The funeral was a small affair, however. Bud was there. And Fred. Most of the rest of the Bowles family attended as well, including Bill, who had been employed by the Madame right up until the day she died.

Suzy was not present, though that was no fault of hers. No doubt she would have come, had she been able. It can be difficult to get away when you're headlining in Moscow.

☆☆☆

Two months after the funeral, Fred left the house early in the morning. He took off, like always, down the road, before anyone awoke. In his hands he held flowers, fancy hothouse ones he'd taken care to buy the day before. He walked for a spell over fields and down dirt roads. Finally, up ahead, he approached the graveyard, sitting beside a set of railroad tracks.

Fred stopped cold. A train was parked up ahead. Right smack next to the graves. On its side it read, "Ringling Brothers Circus." Confused, the man approached.

The performers had not remained on the train. Every last one of them had disembarked. They circled a single grave. One of them, a man in an ostentatious coat, was placing a wreath upon a tombstone.

And there, a ways off, sat a woman on an ostrich. She was sitting sidesaddle, and through the mist there was something about her spine that echoed the very spirit of the Madame herself. Fred approached and his grin grew wide.

Seeing him, Suzy gave a little gasp of surprise and slipped effortlessly off Gaucho's back. She gave Fred an enormous hug, and he thought back to the articles about her he'd

clipped so carefully over the years. "The Ostrich Queen of Middle America." Or, less ostentatiously, "Ostrich Gal?" Even over her shoulder he spied a poster painted on the side of a train car showing a singular young lady leaping a six-foot fence on the back of an ostrich. Sidesaddle. Always side-saddle.

Without a word, Suzy took his hand and, before he could protest, led him over to where one of the elephants was standing, patiently. She lifted his hand, now racked with rheumatism and arthritis, gnarled like the roots of a bristlecone pine tree, to the equally wrinkled elephant's face. Fred stared into the elephant's eye, not noticing when Suzy left his side and walked to the Madame's grave. Not noticing as she placed an object on its top.

But he noticed when she and the ostrich returned to the train. When the circus climbed aboard again, and he had that funny feeling of happiness mixed with the fear of being left behind. Suzy waved goodbye from a window moments later, while Gaucho, jealous for her attention, stuck his own head out the window beside her. Fred saluted them both, then turned to the grave. Before they were out of earshot, he heard Suzy call something.

"Keep it safe for me!"

Later he went to leave his offering, then paused. Lying

on the grave was a single silver brooch in the shape of a woman riding a horse. He picked it up, kissed it, and placed it deep within his breast pocket. Then he started his slow, loping walk for home. He was in no rush. He knew what he'd find when he got there.

About the Madame

☆

All families have stories. Sometimes those stories actually turn out to be true. In my own family, there was always a tale about my grandmother's no-good uncle. As it was told to me, he'd skip out on his farm chores to go from Burr Oak, Michigan, to the nearby town of Mendon. Why? He wanted to visit some elderly ex–circus performer and learn tricks to teach the farm horses back home. It was only years later that my mother discovered that there really had been a Madame Marantette (pronounced, believe it or not, *Maran-tat*). She really had had prizewinning horses. And better still, she'd had ostriches.

World records are made to be broken. Yet to this day, Madame Marantette holds the high jump record for riding side-saddle. She also has maintained the distance record for any person in a surrey pulled by both a horse and ostrich. No one knows how the Madame got it to work in the first place. I have offered my own spin on the events, but her techniques remain as unknowable to us today as they did back then.

To the best of my abilities, I have kept the details of Emma Peek's life as accurate as possible. I should note, however, that while this book indicates that she died around 1930, she

actually died in 1922. That said, Emma Peek did escape her midwestern roots. She married a rich local boy, then seemingly had the marriage annulled but got to hold on to his last name. She traveled the world, joined circuses, performed for kings, and then came back home to Mendon. She and her second husband, Daniel H. Harris, adopted two children, Frances and Arthur, who were also circus performers. She was a

Madame Marantette of Mendon is home for the winter with her trained ostrich "Gaucho." A notice appeared in the Mendon paper warning to the public to keep away from the pasture lot where "Gaucho" is kept, for the bird is in a vicious mood.—White Pigeon New.

legend in her day, and she remains a legend now. A woman with guts and poise, who conquered the world the way she wanted to.

One game I like to play is to spot the brooch at the neck of the Madame. In almost every photograph I've found of her, it's there.

About Bud Thurskow

☆

It is unfortunate that very little information is available about Bud Thurskow, the groom who helped to tend the Madame's horses for around nine years. In this book, I wanted Bud to have his own background story, so I took some inspiration from the history of the great Jimmy Winkfield. Originally, most jockeys in professional horse races in the United States, especially in the South, were Black. It was a job that required knowledge and talent and could make you a good living. Once white people realized this fact, they eventually took those jobs away. Winkfield was the last Black jockey to win the Kentucky Derby, but his life didn't stop there. He went on to win prizes overseas, witness the Russian Revolution, and lose his French estate to the Nazis in 1941. After the war he operated his own racing stable, passing away in 1974 at the age of ninety-two.

Jimmy Winkfield

How to Ride Sidesaddle

☆

Nothing could be simpler! Allow the Madame's adopted daughter, Florence Harris Mardo, to show you. Here she is in a series of photographs.

You simply . . .

Then you . . .

And finally you . . .

See? Easy-peasy!
Now, you try.

Bringing the Madame to Life

☆

When I was a child growing up in Kalamazoo, Michigan, there was a famous illustrator who lived not too far from my town. If you grew up in the 1980s, then you probably knew David Small best for his book *Imogene's Antlers* (featured on *Reading Rainbow*!), about a girl who wakes up to find antlers growing from her head. I remember one day in fourth grade, David himself came to Parkwood-Upjohn Elementary School and spoke and drew pictures for us in the library. My mom worked in the Athena Book Shop (now sadly out of business) and knew him well enough that I could occasionally meet him. Not that I'd say much. I was shy with regular grown-ups, let alone those in the award-winning illustrator category.

One day, my mother found out from a Mendon couple that David lived in a house that belonged to Madame Marantette. Mom put two and two together and told me that our old family story now connected us directly to David Small.

People ask where a person might get an idea for a book.

I think I can safely say that this piece of information sat untouched in my little gray cells for a very long time. I grew up and became a children's librarian, but I never quite forgot that David Small lived in a house connected to a woman who, in turn, had a tenuous tie to my family.

I decided it would make a good picture book. How neat would it be to do a book featuring that no-account lazy uncle and the Madame, and to perhaps ask David Small to take a stab at the art? So I came up with a story involving a kind of child stand-in for one of my grandmother's sisters (who, alas, never did run away to join the circus, though she did hightail it to Detroit) and sent it off to David. He read it and invited me to his house so that we could talk. I had a marvelous time seeing David's studio, as well as the gardens of Sarah Stewart (David's wife), and meeting with the historian Holly Stephenson, who gave us all the information you could possibly want about the Madame. But, of course, David didn't see this book as a picture book at all. He saw it as a novel. And he believed that I could write it.

Clearly, if you are reading this book, it is because of David Small. No one else could have brought it to life. No one else believed in it so strongly before it existed. No one else could have illustrated it. Thank you, David.

Acknowledgments

☆

Books don't just spring from the head of the author, like Athena from her father's skull, fully formed and ready to do battle with the world. I have always been of the opinion that a book should be similar to the credits of a movie. There should be a big section at the end that mentions everyone, from the editor, copy editor, designer, and other in-house folks to the people who helped with the research, ideas, feedback, and so on. Heck, if I had my way, I'd put the names of my agent and my editor on the cover of the book, side by side with my own. In a fair world, that is.

But seeing as how this world is sometimes anything but fair, the best I can do is to thank them here. And my first thanks go to David Small himself, of course. If the Madame's story has been told in any way, he is the true reason why. Thanks, too, to my agent, Stephen Barbara, who is the king of perfect timing. He knows precisely when it is the right moment to pitch a book, and his feedback is key. As I told him with this one, I hope I've finally justified my place on your list. My editor, Erin Clarke, was kind enough to take a chance on an ostrich gal, and for that I am truly grateful. My slim little manuscript acquired big, bulky muscles after her notes. Notes, I should say, that I pretty much agreed with, every step of the way. How lucky is an author to find that in an editor, eh?

So much of the research for this book simply could not exist without the overwhelming generosity of Holly Stephenson of the St. Joseph County Historical Society. When writing a fictionalized narrative of a real person like the Madame, you know you will have a great deal of research to do. So imagine what it is like to meet with a historian and for her to place in your arms a thick folder brimming with all the research you could possibly want (and that probably exists) on the subject. Holly saved me hours and hours of work with that extraordinary gift. I hope I have done the Madame justice in return.

Thanks to Bonnie Jo Campbell, perhaps the greatest novelist of rural Michigan, for her 1920s fencing research.

For my husband, Matt, and my kids, Lillian (who helped considerably with her handwriting samples) and Jack. Thank you for allowing me the chance to disappear for long periods of time into the past, only coming up for the occasional breath of air and iced chai latte.

For my family—my mom and Aunt Judy and our Burr

Oak relatives—thank you for not only editing this book within an inch of its life but also allowing me to cannibalize our history. Famous family lines like "Ain't got enough blood to bleed to death" are too good not to write down. Thanks for letting me take liberties with our history. You all know what parts are true and what parts are made up. I'm glad I could share them with the rest of the world.

And finally, if you want to know even more amazing facts about ostriches, you don't have to grab a book from the nineteenth century. *The Superpower Field Guide: Ostriches* by Rachel Poliquin, with art by Nicholas John Frith, is probably the best kids' guide to ostriches you are ever going to find. You simply cannot read it and not want to know more about these keen, kooky, modern-day dinosaurs. See, that's how you know when a book is written by a librarian. They're just going to recommend you go out and read another book right afterwards. Ha!